Her Sacred Scars

Based on a true story

Sarah Harper

Copyright © 2023 by Sarah Harper
All rights reserved. No part of this book may be copied
or reproduced in any form.
without written permission from the Author.

Dedications

I would like to dedicate this book to everyone I have written about and included in this book. Thank you all, for being part of my journey in whichever you have entered or exited my life. You have helped me to learn and grow in more ways than you may know. I am grateful for your teachings. You have taught me how to move beyond my fears and helped me step into the greatest love story towards myself. Thank you, for being my muses of inspiration.

Prefix

She was certain she would be found by the loud beating of her heart that tried to escape her chest.

Boom. Boom. Boom. Boom.

"Open the door!" She heard the woman scream along with the pounding on the bathroom door which seemed extra loud this time.

She pulled her legs as tightly as she could toward her body. Fears of the familiar sounds on the other side of the door kept her crippled in the tiniest ball she could place herself in. As she hid in the complete darkness of the upstairs bathroom closet.

All she wanted to do was to run as fast as she could to find help but already knew her voice would not be heard. They never believed her all the other times this happened. Why would they? She was only eight years old.

Be as still and be as quiet as you can be she thought, as she knew it would all be over shortly.

As the banging on the door gradually started to fade away, she heard her mother's footsteps stumble back downstairs.

A few more minutes in here for safety, she thought. She began to release her tightly woven grip from around her legs.

Those minutes always felt like hours to her.

As the house became silent, she quietly began to search her way out to locate the closet doorknob.
She became an expert at not making a sound. She had learned to move around silently. Her ears always attentive for any sudden noise around her in case she would have to hide again.

She inched her way to grip the bathroom door handle and very slowly opened it.

Silence.

She knew she was safe for the time being and that it wouldn't be long until she found her mother passed out somewhere in the house.

She steadily walked through the upstairs hallway and made her way down the carpeted stairs making sure to avoid the ones that made noise.

The silence persisted.

Each calculated step she took brought her into her mother's bedroom where she laid in a puddle of her own vomit. This was all too familiar to Mia.

Chapter One

Her own screams had woken her again. Her heart speedily galloped. Her breath was shallow and rapid. She felt her tears rapidly stream down her face and the coldness from the puddle of sweat she laid in that had soaked through her pajamas and onto her sheets.

3:17 am

Mia bent her knees and moved into a fetal position to catch her breath to process yet another nightmare. Except these nightmares were not nightmares but the familiar memories of her childhood experiences that kept haunting her.

She took a long deep breath to help her release the intrusive feelings of fear that she was trying to escape from her mind and body.

I am safe now, she thought to herself. I am in my own bed. My own home. I am safe.

She felt her feet sway off the edge of her bed to sit.

Her heart still raced.

Breathe.

With one hand on her heart and the other on her stomach, she felt into her body so she can connect with the present moment.

Ease finally washed over her, and she felt her shoulders begin to drop as she released the tension from the barriers of protection her body was once used to installing.

She reached for her night table and grabbed the glass of water beside her.

She felt the room-temperature water touch her soft lips and took a sip.

Another breath and the onset of peace began to enfold her body.

She lifted the covers and moved to the other side of the bed in the empty space where it was once occupied by her former husband. She was too tired to change her sheets. *I'll do it at sunrise* she thought to herself and rolled on her side to try and fall back asleep.

Her sleep was not the same anymore.

Her mind was still attached to the old parts of her life. Her doubts. Her fears. The questions she asked herself over the past few months and her life-changing decisions she had made. To leave a picture-perfect life that she felt confined to and pursue a path of self-discovery. A path towards her freedom. But the memories of her past and her former husband still consumed her. The life they had created together and the years of hollowness she felt within her heart for the love she had longed to receive.

Her eyes opened once more to see the numbers on her phone.

4:47 am.

She took another deep breath and closed her eyes. *Breathe,* she thought to herself and felt her body try to loosen its hold before falling asleep once more.

Chapter Two

Mia felt a vibration beneath her head from her phone's alarm that she had left under her pillow.

5:15 am.

She jumped out of bed and used the bathroom before walking down the hall of her rental house.

She was grateful to have found this temporary home until she was able to get back on her feet. Her separation happened only four months ago, and she was still trying to adjust to her new life without him.

She had been with him for so long that she had forgotten who she was without him.

Mia placed her right hand on the wooden railing and felt the wintry hardwood steps on the bottoms of her feet as she descended the staircase towards her living room.

She walked over to the thermostat to check the temperature. Only twenty degrees Celsius. *This is too cold for February* she thought and increased the temperature by two degrees.

She walked into her kitchen to make herself a coffee. This morning was different. Mia was filled her with a new sense of excitement as she was anticipating the trip she was leaving for the next morning.

It would be the first time she would travel alone. She never vacationed solo before as she was always too scared to or married. She had only ever traveled without him once and that was with her sister and girlfriend, so it didn't even count.

But this trip was different. She was on her way to reconnect with the new lover she had recently met at work.

She opened her cupboard, reached for her favourite gold mug, and poured herself a coffee with a splash of coconut milk. She felt a smile on her face and gently bit her bottom lip as she reminisced over the first time they met.

It was instantaneous. The moment her blue eyes met with his seductive brown eyes she felt the pull. Like someone had placed a magnet in her heart that was pulling her closer to his with each breath they took. A coming together of the reunion of two souls.

She smiled again and took a sip of her hot coffee and walked back up the cold steps toward her bedroom. Her hands grabbed the doorknobs to open her closet doors so she could start packing. She reached for her rose gold carry-on suitcase and placed it on the floor.

She thought to herself, *how am I going to fit all my clothes in this small suitcase?* But remembered she would only be gone for three days. She didn't require many items.

She took her newly bought black lace thongs along with some other pieces of lingerie from her top drawer and neatly folded them and placed them in the bottom of her luggage.

She packed her final articles of clothing in her suitcase and walked into her bathroom and began to remove her clothes. She reached to turn on the shower to the hottest setting she can handle and stepped in to indulge in the warmth of the running water.

11:37 am

A missed text message from her lover.

Less than twenty-four hours. I can't wait.

She still felt his magnetic pull. But this time it felt stronger since his absence. He came to work here on a contract for a few months and only met him during his last month of work. She missed seeing him and how he felt.

She remembered the night after the first time their eyes locked that day at work. She had a brief conversation with him regarding a paper, and when she went to lay in bed that night, it was as though she felt him lying right there in the bed next to her.

She turned the water off and wrapped herself in a towel to dry off before putting on her clothes on and making her way back down the staircase. This time the steps didn't feel so cold.

She opened her computer and sent off the last work emails she had to complete before secretly leaving for another country to spend the next few days with her lover.

The sun was shining brightly onto her computer through her windows. *A beautiful winter* day she thought. She had completed all she needed to do before she left, so, she decided to grab her warm plush jacket and bundle up to go outside for a nice snowy walk

Chapter Three

The wind felt frigid on her cheeks, but the warmth of the sun seemed to melt the cold away.

She loved to walk and connect with nature and walked in the direction of her favourite hideaway close to her home. A pond where not too many people went to visit and a place she was never found.

As she strolled along the icy sidewalks towards her favourite secret spot, thoughts quickly filled her mind with all the judgments and gossip she had recently endured.

A month after the news broke out, Mia sat down with her sister and asked her if she had heard from their father about her recent decision to leave her marriage of fifteen years.

A forever ingrained in Mia's mind. The moment

of disapproval she saw in her sister's eyes, followed by

her cutting words, "do you know how many days I cried over this news when I found out? All my friends and I think you are making the biggest mistake of your life and leaving a perfect marriage."

Mia was left momentarily speechless, trying to register what she had just heard.

It made no sense in Mia's mind why everyone else cared so deeply about her life. Her decisions. Why the hell did it matter so much to them anyways? The decisions were hers to make. Not theirs.

"Do you want to ask me how I am doing?" Mia asked in confusion, trying to withhold her tears.

The only replies that came out of her sister's mouth were more irrational comments and criticisms.

But the scars from her sister's stabbing words along with the judgement from the panel of people remained. For now.

Mia knew in her heart that breaking her idea of a 'til death do us part' was the hardest decision she was ever faced with and did not need to try and justify her choices to anyone. She never intended to hurt the man she married, but the walls of confinement she felt in that relationship, she could no longer sustain. She felt half-dead inside for far too long, from the emotional disconnection and loneliness with her former spouse, she knew she had to leave. Something her sister and others could not understand.

Since childhood, the gap between Mia and her sister grew. Mia felt that their childhood trauma from trying to escape their alcoholic mother and the authorities not listening to their cries before their parents' divorce, had left deep lasting wounds that could not be repaired.

Mia always felt an energy of jealousy that seemed to have loomed between her and her sister. Some sort of energy of competition. But Mia was never about competing. For Mia, it was always about being able to have felt loved and accepted by her. A love Mia longed for from her sister. A love she knew she would not be able to receive. Not now. Maybe even ever.

Chapter Four

Mia could hardly sleep. Her excitement to be in her lover's arms once more coursed throughout her entire body. All she could think about was him.

She thought back to their first encounter. There was no kiss. Just the beating of their hearts that fell in sync with each other. Her heart raced and butterflies swirled around her stomach when he pulled her close to hold her against his body in the pouring rain late that evening. Through their wet clothes and drenched hair, the magnetic forces that pulled them together, felt as though it had come to a stop. In unison. Together. Aligned, and complete.

Mia craved this feeling of this forceful pull to reunite since its absence. She undressed and walked into her bathroom and started the water for a warm shower.

She paused in front of her mirror and looked at her naked self with anticipation of his hands and lips touching every inch of her body. She smiled with arousal and leaned over to turn on the hot shower knowing she would soon feel his naked body all over hers.

Her shower was interrupted by the chiming of a text message.

See you soon lover xo.

She smiled once more as she read his text and replied, **can't wait to feel your lips on mine. See you when I land, sexy.**

Mia looked at the time.

8:12 am

She turned off the shower and rushed to put on her thin black lace thongs and matching pushup bra, a pair of blue tight jeans, and a tight black long-sleeve top.

She placed her last few items in her carry-on bag and made her way to her car where nobody except her lover knew where she was going.

Her nerves kicked in as she remembered she would be traveling alone.

She finished getting ready and placed her final belonging in her trunk and drove through rush-hour traffic.

Mia arrived at the correct terminal and made her way easily through customs and found her gate.

That was way easier than I thought it would be, she thought to herself.

She sat down and waited until her boarding number was called, then made her way onto the plane to her assigned seat, beside the window of a half-empty plane.

Ease washed over her, and she now felt relaxed knowing she was halfway there and settled on the plane.

She felt the vibration of the engines start and the aircraft reverse to make its way to the runway. Mia looked out the window and watched another plane take off before she felt the strong oscillating movement of her airplane speed down the runway and into the sky for takeoff.

Her eyes peeled to the exterior of the window as she watched the buildings below become smaller and smaller. She faintly heard the captain's announcement that the seatbelt sign had now been turned off before she closed her eyes and quickly fell asleep.

Her dream quickly took her back to when she was on a flight to the south of France with her friend Morgan.

Morgan was a flight attendant and had asked Mia if she wanted to go to France with her. A girls-only trip. A first for Mia, as she had never attempted to travel without her former spouse during her marriage.

Mia had met Morgan seven years earlier and they had become inseparable over the years. She felt more like what a sister should feel like to Mia. Someone who she could have belly laughs with and share her deepest secrets with.

Suddenly, Mia felt the squeezing grip of anger from Morgan's hand placed around her left arm.

"How could you do this?" Blurted Morgan. "This is not the Mia I know! How could you even think of leaving your marriage? The Mia I know would fight for her marriage."

Her dream abruptly shifted to her former husband who stood beside Morgan, who was also yelling at Mia "You are abandoning me, just like your mother abandoned you!"

Mia jolted awake. Her breathing was heavy. She quickly looked around to see if anyone had noticed the terror on her face.

Mia touched her arm as she thought back to where the bruising had marked her skin the day after the incident.

She took a deep breath and fought back her tears as this was not only a dream but the last encounter she had with Morgan.

She closed her eyes to gather her thoughts and took a few more deep breaths before looking out the plane window. She could now see the sun hitting the beautiful peaks of the white mountain tops below that were covered in snow.

Despite what happened between Mia and Morgan, she was forever grateful for her trip to France. That trip was the trip that planted the seed in Mia's heart for her to create a new life and to fulfill her heart's biggest desires. A life of adventures, of love, romance, freedom, and new beginnings.

She heard the captain's voice over the muffled speaker, "Ladies and gentlemen, Colorado welcomes you. The local time is 4:49 pm. For your safety and the safety of those around you, please remain seated with your seat belt fastened and keep the aisles clear until we are parked at the gate.

Chapter Five

Mia reached for the overhead bin above her head and grabbed her suitcase and placed it on the floor. She walked down the narrow aisle and exited onto the jet bridge. Her heart started to flutter as she made her way through the tunnel and into the airport.

She took her phone out of her purse and sent him a message letting him know that she had landed and was making her way to the arrivals pickup zone.

Be there in 5 minutes beautiful. I can't wait to kiss your lips! Look out for a black Lexus SUV. Was his reply.

She stopped at the washroom where she opened her carry-on and took out her makeup for some last-minute touch-ups and re-applied her lip gloss before putting everything away.

She glanced at herself one last time in the mirror and smiled with self-approval and left to find the signs that led her outside to the arrivals section.

The exit doors automatically opened to a bright warm sunlight she felt on her face and took a deep breath with the fresh Colorado air. She looked around but didn't see him or his black Lexus.

She walked closer to the curb to be more visible and felt her body slightly tremble with nervousness and exhilaration.

Breathe, she thought to herself.

As she waited, she watched the different cars come and go as they picked up their loved ones.

Mia's heart raced as she felt the pulling force of their energies being reunited when she saw his black Lexus SUV driving towards her.

He parked his car in front of her and got out to walk around the back of his vehicle towards her. Their eyes locked and a huge smile appeared on his face.

She stood anxiously on the ledge of the sidewalk and smiled back at him as he approached her at eye level.

"I missed you," he told her and wrapped his arms around her waist and pulled her right up against his body.

"Me too," she replied and felt his lips touch hers with his seductive energy pouring onto her from his embrace.

"I'm so happy you came, and I can't wait to get you back to my place so I can take off your all clothes." He softly whispered in her ear.

He released his hold from her and opened the passenger side door gesturing for her to get in and sit down. He then grabbed her luggage and placed it in his trunk.

He got in the driver's side door and sat down. Adam looked into her blue eyes, and he gently took her left hand to kiss it.

"Ready?" He asked her. Mia nodded in agreement then he put the car in drive.

She tried her best not to stare at him as they drove, but his gaze kept meeting hers.

His salt-and-pepper hair was perfectly in place to match his perfectly groomed salt-and-pepper beard. His black-framed glasses magnified his deep brown flirtatious eyes.

"You'll love it here, "he said and kissed her hand once more. "I'm only twenty minutes away."

He was right, she immediately fell in love with the scenery. It was breathtakingly beautiful with all the mountain peaks covered in snow that surrounded the homes along the streets. It was hard not to instantaneously fall in love with this place and all its picturesque views.

"This is my street." He pointed to the right and she looked at the steep road up the mountain toward his house.

He pulled into a driveway on the left and pushed a button that opened the garage door.

"We can get your suitcase later." He said in a seductive tone. "I want you so badly" And kissed her lips.

"I want you too." She said softly under her breath.

As they exited the cars, the intensity of their sexual desires for each other was unstoppable. He firmly grabbed her face and kissed her again then fumbled for his keys and unlocked the door to his house.

He let her walk in first and tenaciously spanked her ass. She turned back towards him to meet his lips with hers. She then felt his hands reach down to untuck her shirt from her pants and lifted it off over her head.

He pulled her half-naked body against his as he caressed her again. He began to move his lips down her neck and onto her breasts.

"You are so sexy", he whispered and took her hand to lead her upstairs toward his bedroom.

Their naked bodies enveloped each other with the panting of their breath and the beating of their hearts.

He laid her on his bed and climbed on top of her. She felt the weight of his body on hers, thrusting, moving deep inside of her body. She moaned with pleasure as he stared into her blue eye again and smiled.

"You feel so good." He said and climaxed with her.

He covered their naked bodies with a blanket and pulled her close into his arms. She felt his hand gently brush away the blonde hair that covered her face.

"You must be hungry?" He asked.
"Starving," she replied.

"Let's get dressed so I can take you out to dinner." He told her. "But first, let me go grab your suitcase."

She wrapped a blanket around her while she waited for Adam to bring her belongings.

"Here, you can have the guest room all to yourself to get ready. I was thinking something casual tonight since it's already late."

"That sounds perfect. Thank you, handsome," Mia replied and placed her luggage on the spare bed in the guest room.

She opened her bags and put on her skinny jeans and white blouse and unbuttoned it to show just enough cleavage and touched up her makeup.

There, she thought. *All set.*

"Are you ready? he asked as he slowly opened the door hoping to get a glimpse of her before she put her clothes back on.

"I'm all set to go!" she said as she grabbed her purse.

"How do you feel about nachos and guac?" He asked.

"As long as they have margaritas to go with it, I'm in!" She replied.

Chapter Six

As they pulled out of his driveway, he reached for her hand to hold it and gave it another kiss.

This time, she couldn't see his seductive eyes because of the night sky that was filled with stars.

He turned up the music and they drove off.

She recognized his love for music. He would often send her songs in messages as a way of expressing how he felt about her.

He was a quiet man and kept his emotions to himself. He was very meticulous and loved to analyze every detail about every situation with all possible outcomes before making any decisions.

Something she wasn't used to in her previous relationship. She seemed to be the one who was forced to be the decision-maker, the planner, and the caregiver. A task she didn't always love or want.

Over the years, Mia became resentful and depleted in her marriage trying to repair their connection and her fight to communicate her needs that she so desperately wanted reciprocated.

She tried to think back to when these emotions arose within her and her relationship with her former spouse Jack but couldn't recall a defining moment.

It was something that just happened over time. She had just given up after many years of failed attempts. Her love for Jack began to fizzle away years before she had left him even though she had tried to honour her promise to him, to them, and their wedding vows.

Mia desperately wanted to feel wanted and desired. To feel loved and admired again. To be taken care of by a prince charming.

That's when the Universe inserted Adam into her life. That was the moment she had new hope. That there was in fact such a thing as a prince charming.

"We're almost there babe." He said as she could see his shadowy face in the darkness turn towards her.

He parked the car and they walked into his go-to neighbourhood Mexican restaurant.

"Hi, Adam!" Said one of the wait staff. "Right this way." She escorted them to a booth over on the bar side.

"The usual beverage?" She asked Adam.

"Yes, thank you, and she will have the same. Spicy Margarita, right?" And looked and Mia for her approval.

"That would be wonderful! Thank you." She replied and watched the waiter leave to place their order.

"I still can't believe you're here! I have to keep touching you to make sure that this is real." As he reached over to hold her hand that was resting on the table.

"I love how you hold my hand!" And took his hand to bring it to her lips to kiss him.

"Here's your Spicy Margaritas." The waitress said placing the drinks in front of them.

"I'll give you a few more minutes before I place your food order."

Adam raised his glass, "Cheers, babe! To you being here with me!"

Mia could not remember feeling this kind of exhilaration before. After all, she had left her country without telling anyone to go visit a man she had only known for a few months.

But it felt right. Her gut always guided her, and she always listened to her inner nudges, even when it didn't make any sense to her.

All she knew was that she wanted to spend as much time as she could with this man, to get to know him more, and make passionate love with him while she explored her re-ignited sensual side that had been dormant for many years.

"Ready to place your food order now?" Asked the waitress when she returned.

"Yes! We'll share nachos and quac, a house salad, and some tacos for two please."

"I'll be right back with your order." Replied the waitress and left once again.

They laughed as they shared more stories while sipping on their margaritas before their food arrived.

The food was delicious, but they had ordered way more than they could finish.

"I know it's getting late for you, especially with the time

change and all. How would you like to soak in my hot tub while we stare at the stars when we get back to my place?" He hoped.

"That sounds amazing." Was her reply and notice him licking his lips in anticipation to have her for dessert.

"Let's go then, beautiful." He said, then he paid the bill before leaving to go back to his place.

The drive back was another beautiful sight to be seen as there were not a lot of streetlights and she could see the clear night sky filled with stars.

When they arrived back at his place, they entered through the garage and into the kitchen. He grabbed two wine glasses from the cupboard. "You prefer white wine, correct?" He asked as he grabbed a bottle of each a red and a white.

"Yes, please." She responded.

"Why don't go get undressed. I'll have this ready for you when you are done." He said as he kissed her and gently pushed her away towards the direction of the bedroom.

Thankfully, Mia thought about packing her bikini. She put it on and headed back down the staircase towards the living room, Adam was standing there wearing his robe. He was holding a second one for her. She slid into it.

He opened the sliding door that led them to the concrete patio. Mia felt the chilly air on her feet and face as she followed Adam outside towards the hot tub.

She saw him place the glasses of wine on a little table just beside the jacuzzi.

"You go first so I can take your robe." He insisted. This was the kind of thoughtfulness she had been desiring. She felt his hands touch her shoulders to remove it from her body.

She climbed in and sat down in the right corner. It was the perfect temperature.

She watched him undo the belt on his robe and could see his fully naked body through the opening. He handed her their wine glasses of wine and then tossed his robe on top of the side table.

For a moment she felt almost embarrassed that she had worn her bathing suit.

She watched him climb in and moved towards her. She felt his soft lips meet hers and he grabbed his wine glass from her hand and placed it on the ledge. He guided her half-dressed body towards his naked torso and pulled her to sit on his bare lap. Her back rested against his lightly hairy chest and her buttocks slid against his upper thighs and she felt his hands wrap around her waist.

"I love having you in my arms." He whispered in her ear.

"This is the perfect night. It's even more beautiful with you here by my side and all the stars shining down upon us."

She liked the sounds of his words and started to envision a new life here. With him. With all of this.

"It couldn't be any more perfect!" She whispered back.

She felt his right hand moving back and forth along her waist and descending along her hip and towards her inner thighs.

"You feel so good to me." He whispered again and she felt him slip inside her.

Chapter Seven

3:41 am.

Her eyes were wide awake from all the excitement, but her body felt tired. Mia was never good at adjusting to different time zones and her sleepless nights had become a regular thing since her separation.

She heard his breathing and felt the warmth coming from his naked body as they laid under the soft white duvet with her thoughts running through her mind.

As her walls of betrayal came crumbling down, she saw everything and everyone through a new lens. For the truth of who they really are. Of whom she really is and was. A woman who no longer resonated with those types of people.

The raw accuracy awoke within her vision of how she allowed others to treat her. What others expected or wanted from her, and these superficial relationships that she had, were far from what Mia's heart desired.

It was all based on a story she told herself when she was a little girl. Who she wanted to be when she grew up. From the fairytales she read in books that she longed to recreate in her life. To live with a man and tell their tale of their happily ever after. To abide to other people's needs first over her own. To appear to be perfect in every way. However, to be perfect was to follow the outdated belief systems of others.

What she came to realize, was her emptiness came from within her. That she was this fictional character who poured all her love and devotion into a man and her friendships so much so, she lost her own identity in the process.

She found it much easier to attend to other people's needs over her own because she thought by doing so, she would be loved and appreciated.

It had become a way of being for her. It was all she ever knew.

Until her awakening.

That's when her entire life rapidly changed before her eyes.

One month she lived in her childhood fairytale, the next month she had left her marriage, started a new job, and met an intriguingly seductive and handsome man.

Mia had even prayed for this change for months during her morning prayers and meditations before it actually manifested. She had been visualizing her heart opening to new levels of love. To new wonderful expansive opportunities. She felt this massive change coming. But she didn't know to what capacity.

She felt Adam roll over as her body rested beside him. He continued to sleep. She looked over at him and felt so much gratitude in her heart for her taking this incredible leap of faith towards him.

Chapter Eight

She woke up to Adam softly kissing her forehead.

"Good morning, beautiful." He said his deeply scruffy morning voice that sounded so sexy to her. "How was your sleep?"

"Well, to be honest, I don't sleep much these days. However, I really enjoyed you lying next to me. How was your sleep? You seemed to be well rested?"

"It was great. Normally I don't sleep well with someone beside me. For some reason, I felt so peaceful with you beside me. Thank you."

She felt his arms pull her into him. His soft fingertips ran down her backside. She wrapped her leg around his waist. She kissed him passionately and moved her hips onto top of his.

Hours went by before they got out of bed.

"Coffee?" He asked when they were finished.

"Yes, please. Do you have almond or coconut milk?"

"Bought some almond just for you."

"Why, thank you," Mia replied and gave him another kiss.

"I am going to hop in the shower. I'll be right down." She told him.

She met him on the couch where he had her coffee waiting for her. He looked at his phone and laughed at some kind of funny video.

"After our coffees, I want to take you to a special store. Ok? I am not telling you what kind of store it is. You'll see what it is when we get there." He told her with a smirk on his face.

They finished their coffees and got ready to go to wherever he was taking her. They got in his black SUV and drove down the mountain towards the main road. She had no idea where they were going but loved a good surprise.

It was another beautiful sunny day. The air was cold but not like winter back home. Here, the air felt fresh. The views of the snowy-covered mountains were glorious and stunning. It was all so breathtaking to her.

He turned up the music to a song she hadn't heard before. She had become attentive to the lyrics of any song Adam played or sent to her. She knew they were intentional. She heard the lyrics over the car speakers of a song she was not familiar with, "I think I'm falling in love, this time a think it's for real." She felt his hand move onto her thigh. She looked and him as he quickly took his eyes off the road and smiled at her.

She loved what she felt when she was with him. She couldn't help but feel as though this was all too good to be true.

They pulled up to the front doors of a larger building along a side street. She tried to figure out what the light-yellow brick structure was. It didn't have a big sign out front or many windows. It looked more like a smaller warehouse.

"I'll drop you off here and go park the car. I'll meet you inside." He told her.

She agreed and opened her door with a slightly confused look on her face.

"Ok, see you in there!" He said and drove to the side of the building to park.

As she approached the building, there were two smaller windows beside the solid wood entrance doors. She noticed a few Buddha statues and large amethyst crystals.

When she opened the door, the place was larger than she expected.

It was a spiritual store filled with all different kinds of crystals, sages, singing bowls, tarot decks, and everything she loved!

Her eyes looked over to the left and she saw a long jewelry counter that was filled with a variety of beautiful and unique pieces of precious gemstones.

That's where I'll start, she thought to herself. She began her walk over and saw Adam come through the front door.

"I thought you would like it here!" He said approaching her as he saw a huge smile of delight on her face.

"You know, I've been searching for a specific stone to wear as a ring. This place is perfect! I am going to start looking there." She told him and pointed to the far end to the jewelry counter.

All the stones were colour-coordinated like a magical rainbow that ran along the entire set of cases.

There were so many choices of gems that caught her eyes. She was looking for a Jade stone that would help her heart heal, bring balance and good luck to her on her new life's path.

Mia spotted the green-coloured stones. She was drawn to a uniquely shaped chunkier ring. It was a raw oval-shaped jade stone nestled in the center of two thin silver rings that ran along the top and bottom exterior edges of the stone and merged at the bottom to form a solid band. It reminded her of the evil eye symbol.

"Can I help you with anything?" asked the worker behind the counter.

"I would love to try on that ring, please." Mia pointed to the upper right corner of the holding case.

"This one?" asked the worker.

"That's the one! Thank you." Mia replied to the worker who immediately pulled out the case and placed it on top of the glass counter.

Mia placed the ring on her left middle finger. It fit perfectly.

"Cool ring. Looks good!" He said.

"I think I found the one!" Mia excitedly said and gave it back to the worker to prepare it for her purchase.

"I can look around here all day! This place is so cool! Thank you so much for taking me here." She said and kissed Adam on his lips.

"My pleasure." He kissed her back. "Next, we have to stop at the grocery store. I have to grab a few things for dinner tonight. I was thinking of a nice dinner in. I wanna cook for you."

"Well, I look forward to watching you in action!" She said with a smile.

She paid for her ring and placed it on her finger as soon as they got back into the car.

"Oh, thank you again for taking me to that incredible store! I absolutely love this ring!"

"I am happy you found it. I hope it gives you what you are looking for." He told her.

He always had the perfect thing to say, she thought as he put the car in drive and started to make their way back to his place.

The sun was setting behind the decorative mountain peaks. Each minute that passed while she was there, she was beginning to fall in love with the idea of a fresh start here. Away from everyone back home. Away from all the drama. Her new beginning.

She desired a simple life with the spontaneous adventures that she so craved.

Nothing held her back anymore. She was ready and had been ready for a while now.

They turned right and drove back up the mountain that led to his driveway on the left.

"We're home," he said as he pulled into his driveway and gave her another kiss when he parked.

"Let me help you with the groceries." She told him.

"I got this. You're my guest for the next few days. You deserve to be pampered. I'm taking care of you while you are here."

Her heart fluttered. She was not used to anyone taking care of her this way but was starting to get used to it.

She stood in the kitchen as she watched Adam place the groceries on the counter.

"I'm going to unpack while you have a seat and relax," Adam said and pulled the tall black rounded stool from under the breakfast bar for her to sit.

"You sure you don't need any help?" she asked again.

"I got this! Thank you though," and kissed her.

She watched him open the middle cupboard doors and take out the wine glasses, then placed them in front of her.

He then went over to the opposite side of the kitchen to grab a bottle of red and white wine and carried them over back towards her.

He opened the bottles and poured a glass of white for her and red for him.

"Cheers babe," and he raised his glass to hers, "to new adventures."

They each sipped their wine and exchanged another kiss.

"Now, for me to get started with making us dinner." And he turned his back to walk towards the stove.

"You're sure I can't help you?" She insisted.

"I can already tell you feel so out of place and uncomfortable not taking over my kitchen." He said with a chuckle. "I just want you to sit there and watch me. Talk with me. Have fun with me while I cook. It's your turn for someone to take care of you, and I would love to be that someone." He blew her a kiss and ignited the gas stove.

He was right. Mia felt uncomfortable sitting on his stool. She was aware she felt her frozen-like body from the tightness in her shoulders and the clenching of her jaw. Her legs became almost paralyzed with uneasiness. Any time she felt unfamiliar with anything, her response was fear. When something became uncomfortable, it was felt in her entire body. The freeze response that was engrained in her body from years of trauma, was what others would perceive as normal situations.

Yet, Adam helped her feel comfortable and provided all her wants and needs for her. She realized she didn't know how to receive this love and kindness back. It made her feel awkward.

Adam was a charmer and the first one to ever demonstrate such chivalrous behaviour to Mia. Always holding the door open for her to walk through and now making dinner for her without her lifting a finger.

She took a slow deep breath and reached for another sip of her wine.

"It smells so delicious." She told Adam.

He was making sweet potato gnocchi with a homemade pasta sauce.

"Well, it's the first time I have tried out this recipe, so fingers crossed it tastes as good as it smells." He chuckled.

"Why don't you be the first to try?" He walked over to Mia holding a spoon full of sauce and put it up to her lips for her to taste.

She softly blew on the fragrant-smelling aromas that were coming from the sauce and tried it.

"Wow," she said pleasantly surprised, "this taste just like my Sicilian grandmother's recipe!"

"So glad you like it, babe. It's already ready. Let me get our plates." And off he went to grab two plates from the cupboard and plated their dishes.

He took them over to the breakfast bar where Mia was sitting and placed the plates down, one in front of her and one to the left of her.

"Bon appetite. But I do have to be honest, I can't stop thinking about having you for dessert." He kissed her neck just underneath her ear and quietly whispered, "eat."

As he pulled away, she tenderly grabbed his face back towards hers and gave him a soft, sensual kiss on his lips.

"I can't wait for you to eat me for dessert." She whispered back and reached for her fork to take her first bite of food.

The food was delicious, but she couldn't help feeling so aroused. Wanted. Desired. Sexy.

Her sexual desires had been dormant for so long, she could hardly resist him.

She took her left hand and lightly placed it on his upper thigh.

He looked at her with his pressing desires.

Her hand slowly moved up his thigh as she took another bite of her gnocchi, teasing him with her tongue as she licked her lips with her insatiable appetite.

"Mmmmmm." She hummed with the taste of food on her palate, imagining it was him.
Her hand moved to feel his throbbing hard self under her hand.

"Babe." He said in a low whisper. He could hardly speak.

Their hunger for each other was unstoppable.

He grabbed her hand to stop her. He could no longer withhold her touch.

"Fuck, I want you so badly." He said.

He stood up and drew her into his body and she felt his hands grasp her jaw and his tongue entered her mouth.

She felt his hands move to undo the button on her jeans and unzipped her pants to move the fabric of her thong to the side and slip his fingers inside of her.

Mia moaned. "Oh, Adam."

She felt her wetness slide with his fingers.

He continued to remove her pants and black lace thong.

With one motion, he moved his plate and lifted her bare bottom on the cold granite of his breakfast bar.

"I guess I am having dessert first." he said and proceeded to move his tongue between her legs.

She moaned even louder this time.

"I want you to fuck me!" She said with a heavy breath and pulled his head toward hers as he began to remove his belt buckle and dropped his pants down just enough to enter her and feed her starvation for him.

Chapter Nine

"I'm going to miss you when you're gone." He told her when she opened her eyes to his quiet voice lying next to him in his bed that morning.

Her flight was leaving at 3:30 pm and it was already 10:38 am.

"Last night was incredible!" She replied with a kiss on his lips. "This entire time with you has been incredible." She kissed him again.

She felt his hand brush into her hair and pulled her back towards him. She felt his tongue touch hers and his body mount on top of hers. Her heart skipped another beat. He stopped for a moment and gazed deeply into her blue eyes and kissed her again. She felt his legs spreading hers and his hips thrust up against hers.

She moaned when she felt him penetrate deep inside of her.

Feeling every inch of each other. Exploring each other one last time before she left.

She heard him moan once last time and slowly came to a stop.

Their beating hearts pulsed in synchronistic waves as he laid on top of her and gave her one more kiss before rolling off of her body.

"I should start to pack," she said, "I don't want to be late for my flight.

"You're right. Where did the time go? It's already 11:47 am!" He exclaimed.

They quickly hopped out of bed, and she rushed to pack her belongings.

It didn't take her long. Everything she needed was already in her suitcase.

"You have everything?" He asked her when he saw her walking down the stairs.

"Almost, just one last thing." And she walked back into his bedroom and left a thank you note for him on his bed.

Dear Adam,
Thank you for coming into my life. You helped me re-ignite a flame within me that had been dormant for years. I am so grateful for you, your kisses, and your kindness.
I can't wait to see you again soon.
Xoxo,
Mia

"Ready." Mia told Adam as she exited his bedroom.

"I'll grab your bags." They both walked to the garage. He opened her car door and kissed her before she sat down on the passenger's side, then placed her belongings inside the trunk.

He walked around the car and got in. They were both silent. He put the key in the ignition and reversed the car. There was a sense of heaviness that soon they would be apart. He looked at Mia, grabbed her hand and kissed it.

She took in the gorgeous views one last time as they descended the mountain from his place that overlooked the city and lake.

Her mind raced as they drove onto the freeway of different ideas on how they could make this long-distance relationship work.

But it didn't matter right now. She knew that they would figure it out. Their connection was strong, and she could always feel his energy when he would think about her, even from afar.

He turned up the song he was playing on his phone. Paul McCartney. She remembered hearing her dad play when she was a little girl called "A silly love song."

She smiled to herself because she sensed that he did love her but had yet to express those exact words to her.

She continued to admire the scenic drive back to the airport and noticed the sign on the highway that pointed them in the direction of the airport. They were now only two miles away.

Mia double checked her purse to make sure she had her passport before arriving at the airport and applied some more lip-gloss.

"When do you think we will see each other again?" She looked over at Adam hoping he would say within the next few weeks. "Maybe you can come to visit me next time?" She asked.

"I'm not sure. My schedule for the next little while is pretty slammed. But we'll figure something out." He said in a reassuring voice.

He pulled up to the drop off area for the departure flights and stopped along the curb.

They each got out of his car and walked toward the trunk. He lifted her luggage out, placed it on the curb, then grabbed her by her waist.

"I'm really going to miss you. I loved having you here with me." He told her.

"Thank you, Adam. I am so grateful for you. For this experience and everything you've done for me. Another new adventure." She replied before having their last kiss goodbye.

She walked towards the terminal and the automatic sliding doors opened. She glanced back at Adam. They smiled and blew each other their final kiss goodbye.

She took a deep breath as she felt the sadness sink

in that her time with him was over.

Mia found her way over to the airline check-in point where the worker behind the counter greeted her.

"How ya'll doing today?" She said with a thick American accent. "Where ya'll flying to today ma'am?"

"Toronto, Canada," Mia replied and handed over her passport.

As the worker punched in her information, a tall husky man with a well-groomed silver beard stood on her right side. He was a loud talker with a deep voice, but kind with his words. He was holding an unusually large rectangular metal carrying case with him that he placed on the weighted conveyer belt beside Mia.

She overheard the gentleman say something about a ruffle and was asked to open the case so the worker could inspect it.

Everyone around her was used to this sort of thing it seemed. It was a common thing to carry firearms in the

United States, which seemed routine from her observations, yet so foreign for a Canadian. She had never been so close to a gun before that she felt her senses become heightened to her surroundings and every move the man made beside her.

She watched the man in her periphery open the case and take a small step back. Mia's heart raced so rapidly, she thought everyone around her could hear its loud thumping. So many thoughts rapidly sped through her mind like what would she do if something terrible happened in that moment.

She was shocked at the calm nature of everyone around her about this massive looking firearm that was within three feet of her. Not one person flinched.

"All set." Said the worker behind the counter and handed Mia her ticket and passport.

"Thank you." She quickly replied and as fast as she possibly could, grabbed her identification and walked away towards the security checkpoint to make her escape.

By the time she got cleared through customs, she still had another hour to pass before her boarding time.

She found a spot by the window to sit and watched the planes land and take off.

All the feelings of the past few days started running through her. She smiled daydreaming of their time together and all the little romantic moments they shared.

It had felt like she had only been sitting for a few minutes when she heard the announcement over the PA system call her flight number that they were now beginning to board.

Mia made sure she had all her belongings before she made her way through the line to board her flight back home.

As she got on the plane and walked down the narrow aisle, found her window seat, and made herself as comfortable as she could. Within minutes, they took flight.

She snuggled as best she could in her chair and opened her phone to look at some of the pictures she took while she was there.

Mia noticed that her and Adam didn't even take a single photo together. It was only of the mountains she had taken.

She thought to herself maybe it was because she was trying to be present with him and forgot all about taking a picture with him. Next time she thought.

And flipped the app to watch a movie she had downloaded for the plane ride.

12:07 am.

They landed at the Toronto International Airport on schedule, and she made her way through the airport and back to her vehicle as fast as she could. It was late. She was tired, and still had another hour drive home.

1:30 am.

She pulled into her driveway. It had been a long day of traveling and all she wanted to do was get her pajamas on and let Adam know she was home safely.

She unlocked her front door and dumped her bags on the floor in the entranceway. She was too tired to carry them upstairs but would do so in the morning.

I'm home babe. Mia text.

Within seconds she heard her phone ding with his reply, **Happy to hear you got home safe. Have a good sleep. Good night.** Followed by a kissy-face emoji.

She responded with the same emoji, threw on her pajamas, and crawled into bed.

Chapter Ten

6:30 am.

Mia woke up to the buzzing of her alarm. She wanted to wake up to get her workout in before her day started and re-adjust to her time zone.

She got out of bed and went right to the kitchen to make herself a coffee. Her body felt more tired than usual as she felt pretty jet-lagged from the last couple of days. But Mia always knew how to push through.

She paused and smiled ear-to-ear as she stood in front of her brewing coffee. She still couldn't believe everything she had experienced these last few days with him, her travels alone, and exploring a new part of the world.

She felt a new sense of freedom and independence she had been looking for. An empowered self that she had begun to love and embody.

She poured herself a coffee with a splash of coconut milk and went to her meditation corner.

She checked in with her heart and felt the expansive energy within her. Mia knew that this was only the beginning.

Her body, still fatigued from her trip, decided to keep her exercise regime to a minimum, then went upstairs to have a soak in the tub.

She turned on the hot water and poured in some Epsom salts with a few drops of lavender essential oils.

It always reminded her of the lavender scents she loved that she smelt during her visits to France.

Mia took off her clothes and dipped her right foot first, followed by her left, before laying down on her back and began to reminisce about her hot tub experience with Adam.

She still felt his body linger as if it was still pressed against hers and his sensual touch that she felt through her entire body.

She couldn't wait to send him a good morning message but was mindful of the time change. She would do so as soon as she finished her bath.

She closed her eyes as her mind floated in the memories with him until she felt the water temperature cooling off. She pressed the plug and drained the water and unhooked her towel to dry her body.

9:52 am.

Was the time when she reached for her phone.

Adam was two hours behind and she couldn't wait any longer to send him a message.

She started to type, Morning **sexy! I missed waking up to you this morning** and pressed send.

She put on her robe, headed back down her staircase, and grabbed her suitcase to start unpacking before going about her day doing laundry, getting groceries, and catching up on emails and phone calls.

4:41 pm.

Mia was getting worried. She still hadn't heard back from Adam.

She typed him another message. **Hey babe, I hope you are having a good day. Just wanted to check in to make sure you are, ok?** Then placed her phone on the kitchen table so she could start to make an early dinner since she hadn't even had lunch.

Something light to eat she thought because she still felt off with her jetlag.

She looked in her fridge to see what she felt like eating. She saw some lettuce, tomatoes, and avocadoes and decided that was what she would eat with a little drizzle of olive oil and a dash of salt and pepper.

She prepared her salad and sat down on her couch to put on a drama TV series she had started to watch before she left for her mini trip.

8:12 pm

Her phone received a notification.

Hey, babe. All good. Busy days. Talk soon. Was his response.

That's it? She thought.

All of the sudden, something felt off in her gut.
It wasn't the response she had hoped for. It felt rather cold and distant.

She was a bit confused. They had such an amazing weekend together, she thought. Her heart sank a little. Perhaps he wasn't feeling the same sense of excitement she was.

She didn't want to think too much about it but also knew she wasn't going to reply again tonight.

She turned off the TV and washed the dishes before heading back upstairs to get ready for bed.

She pulled back her blankets and fell onto her soft mattress. It was always nice to sleep in her bed but tonight she felt alone.

His absence after being with her the past few days felt even more present after his message. A feeling that she didn't feel comfortable with.

Mia had to make herself stop trying to think about his lack of responsiveness and the distance she felt today after their amazing time together. *I'll bring it up with him tomorrow* she thought.

She was too tired and fearful to even give it any more thought. Instead, Mia reached for her phone and searched for a guided meditation to help her fall asleep.

Chapter Eleven

5:00 am

She woke up to her alarm and started her home routine all over again. Coffee, meditation, and workout before heading off to work.

Today, she was working from her office outside of town alongside her coworkers. She thought that it was the perfect way to help distract her thoughts from what had transpired yesterday with Adam.

She got ready and quickly made her way to her car to try and beat the rush hour traffic, cranked up the music to try and drown out her thoughts during her hour-long commute.

She tried so hard to shake the uncomfortable gut feeling she experienced from his short and brief text messages.

It was a feeling she had felt many times before. A feeling that was familiar to her inner knowing.

She recognized it all the way back from her childhood, from all the wounds she felt when her mother left her at the early age of eight. A feeling of abandonment.

She didn't want to believe it though. She would just wait to see how things progress with Adam. Perhaps she was giving it too much thought. *I'm probably overanalyzing* she thought to herself as it was still too early to tell.

She pulled into her work parking lot with a sense of relief that she was there, combined with excitement to see some familiar faces that would help distract her mind.

As the day went on, she debated whether she should reach out to him or not. She thought *not*. *Wait for him to reach out first.*

Her heart felt sad and used even with the idea that it could all be over just as quickly as he came into her life.

It wasn't just about his last text though. It was what her intuition was telling her. Something was different. Something changed overnight.

She heard her phone chime in hopes it was him. Instead, it was her former husband.

I have sent over all the documents to your lawyer.

Is what she read from the pop-up text.

Before Mia responded she made sure to email her lawyer first to verify she received anything.

Two minutes later, her phone rang with her lawyer on the other line.

"Hi Mia, yes, I received the email from your former husband but most of his financial statements are still missing. We still can't move forward on any of this until he discloses everything. He needs to get his own lawyer."

"Thank you, for letting me know. I will call him and let him know." Mia thanked her.

Mia dialed her ex's number.

"Hey. What's up? You got my text, right?" He asked.

"Yes, I did. I also spoke with my lawyer, and she said, that you have not completed your financial statement and that we can't move forward on our separation agreement until you do. We are requesting you hire your own lawyer to help you." Mia said in a firm voice.

"What else do I need to fill out? I sent everything. Why can't yours just do it all? This was supposed to be easy." He snapped.

"I agree. So, let's keep it that way. Get your own lawyer to represent you so we can get this done as soon as possible, please." She begged and hung up the phone.

She was so irritated at this point. She just wanted the papers signed but her ex was not cooperating. All she wanted was to move on from all of it and needed to complete this last piece of the puzzle for her to do so.

She finished a few more letters for her work then packed up and called it a day.

Still nothing from Adam.

She said goodbye to her coworkers and made her way back home, only this time would take her longer because it was now rush-hour traffic.

She sat in her car and put on her seatbelt. She still couldn't let go of what she felt deep inside.

As she drove, she watched the sunset in the distance, and she thought about the sunsets in Colorado with the mountains and how beautiful they were to see.

A tear fell down her cheek.

That knowing she felt deep within her stomach. A disconnection in his energy. She couldn't understand why.

She felt another tear roll down her face and began to question herself and what she did. Did she do something wrong?

She wanted to ask him but didn't want to seem desperate with how she felt.

She had no proof. Only a hunch.

By the time she pulled into her driveway, it was dark.

She wasn't even hungry.

She just wanted to curl up in her bed.

When she got to her bedroom, she quickly took her clothes off and replaced them with her pajamas and hopped into her bed.

Still nothing from him.

Her loneliness felt even greater tonight.

Tears of sadness streamed down her face and onto her pillowcase before falling asleep in her empty bed.

Chapter Twelve

A few days had now passed and still no word from Adam.

She was brokenhearted and confused. She felt used, misled, and was angry at herself because her gut instinct didn't see this coming.

She was grateful it was the weekend and could take a few days to have time to herself plus process everything that had been happening in her life over the past several months.

When she finally had the strength and courage to leave her marriage to begin a new, the new life that her heart longed for, she did not foresee all the people in her life, her friends, and even some family members who had placed such great judgments upon her and left her.

It appeared to be a familiar pattern in her life. To feel as though everyone would just pick up leave her behind, like her mother and her mother's family did when she was eight years old.

Something she would never fully understand.

When Mia was twenty-seven, she did some research and found where her mother was living. She wanted answers about her mother's side of the family and their disappearance from her life.

Unfortunately, her relationship with her mother and that entire side of that family was brief. Her mother's heavy drinking over the years from trying to bury her own traumas had become too toxic for Mia and she had to walk away.

Still, the wounds of feeling abandoned remained. Now, even deeper with her current losses over this past year.

She placed her hand on her chest. She could feel the tight grip in her wounded heart take hold.

Breathe.

She felt a tear stream down her face and fall onto the floor.
She heard a chime tone in the distance. A notification she received on her phone that made her pause.

She walked over to her kitchen counter to see who it was and became nervous to read what Adam wrote.

Hey, you. I recently met someone. Just before you arrived. I really wanted to be honest with you and not mislead you. I loved the time we spent together when you were here. I love your energy. But to be honest, I am not sure how this relationship with you would work being long distance and all. I think I really like this person here and wanted to give her a fair chance. I hope that we can remain friends. You mean so much to me. Xo.

Mia remained frozen. Trying to take in his words.

Didn't want to mislead? What an asshole!

She couldn't believe what her eyes read. All she felt was the pain in her heart and the uncontrollable tears that rolled down her face like pouring rain.

"You ass hole!" She yelled and fell down on the floor in a curled-up ball.

She couldn't even respond. She had no words. Only pain.

The shock. The betrayals she couldn't bear in her heart anymore. Not with him. Not with anyone else.

Did he not feel the love she felt? What she thought they both felt for each other? Was it all a lie?

But it couldn't have been. She felt it in her heart.

She knew he had wounds from his past relationships but to give this one up with her so easily. She could not make any sense of it.

All she could do was lay there and cry with her pain.

An hour had passed before she reached for her phone to reply to his text.

Thank you for everything. I wish you all the best. And hit the send button.

She didn't want to argue with him or try to convince him as to why he should be with her. She believed wholeheartedly in free will and that she didn't want to interfere with whatever life choices he made with or without her.

Her chest hurt from the daggers of betrayal she felt that had just punctured her heart once more.

She unsteadily walked up her stairs and into her bathroom where she turned on the faucet to have a bath to try to soothe her.

A nice hot bath to kill the pain she thought and poured some lavender essential oils into the water to help calm her nerves.

She started to undress and looked at herself in the mirror.

Maybe I am not pretty enough?

Maybe I am not fit enough for him?

Maybe I am not good enough for him?

All the negative self-talk filled her mind. The voice of her inner critic felt loud and destructive.

Perhaps that voice was right. *There must be something wrong with me if no one wants to be with me.*

Mia walked back over to the tub. The hot water was filling up fast and the steam from the heat was already fogging up the mirror to block her view of herself and her naked body.

It's probably for the best so I can stop criticizing myself, she thought. She placed her right foot into the hot water followed by her left. She was a creature of habit. Trying to replicate all the same movements as she moved through life and her little daily to-do's. Something that brought her comfort.

She laid down in the lavender scented water and the tears began to flow uncontrollably again dropping into the water like pellets of hard rain.

She grabbed her knees and pulled them close to her body, just like she did as a little child. Instead, this time, she no longer wanted to quiet and hide.

This time, she needed to let it all out.

"Ffffuuuuuccckkkkkkkkkkk yyyooouuuuuuuu, you, you, fucking assssssssshooooolllllle!" She screamed so loud she was certain her neighbours could hear.

Chapter Thirteen

Another two weeks had gone by since the last time she had spoken or even heard from Adam.

Mia kept herself busy by focusing on her healing. She had been on her spiritual journey for many years now. She used all the lessons from all her ups and downs, and her life's triumphs and tragedies, and transformed them to learn, heal, grow, and inspire.

Her first spiritual awakening began in her early twenties after many years of experiencing darkness from her childhood traumas.

In her adolescent years, Mia was left angry and confused by the absence of her mother and was always on the search to feel what love and acceptance would feel like.

When she was thirteen, her father remarried. She had hoped that this woman would give her the love she needed from a mother.

Instead, it gave her more heartache. More feelings of not being wanted.

When Mia would return home from school, she would see this woman sitting on her glider chair watching her favourite soap operas. Mia would say "hello" to her as she entered the front door. Mia was always received with a cold icy stare back from her with no reply, as if Mia didn't even exist. She told her dad about it, but he did nothing.

Mia felt worthless and started to isolate herself in her early teens. She would either hide in her room or would lie about going to a friend's house to study, and instead, go off to get drunk or high.

Mia started smoking cigarettes when she was thirteen and had her first encounter with drugs and alcohol by the age of fourteen. The beginning of her addictions.

She only felt wanted when she got the attention from boys that were in their late teens. It made her feel worthy.

One of the guys from the group even invited her to his place one Saturday night. He was throwing a party.

Mia lied to her dad and told him she was staying over at a girlfriend's house. That they had to work on a school project. Instead, she took the city bus downtown to meet this older boy where he lived.

It was a smaller group of guys and two other girls that the party. They started drinking right away. It was the first time Mia ever drank. They poured her a glass of vodka and orange juice, and just like an experienced drinker, she began to chug several drinks.

She was very naïve and ended up unable to sit or even walk by herself. She remembered a couple of the older boys helped her lie down onto a bed at some point throughout the night and put her on her side, so she didn't choke, just in case she threw up.

As she went in and out of consciousness, she vaguely remembered one of the guys from the party rubbing his hands over her lifeless body. Feeling her. Fondling her in front of everyone. No one said a word or tried to stop it, and Mia was too drunk to fight back.

She blacked out the rest of the night and woke up around six o'clock in the morning in her own vomit. Everyone was passed out around her, so she quickly made her escape and took the bus home as if nothing happened. She never told anyone about it, or ever saw that group again.

The more pain she experienced in her life, the more she wanted to become numb to it all.

Throughout her teens, Mia's addictions grew. She was broken inside and became an expert on how to function and act normally around others when she was drunk or high.

Outwardly, Mia appeared happy, and everyone always commented on what a beautiful girl she was.

One night, she was at her friend's house celebrating her friend's birthday. They had all gone out to the bar and were all hammered and high, like usual, laughing and having a good time.

They all returned to her friend's house for more drugs and drinks. After all, the night was still young to them.

Her friend's boyfriend kept hitting on Mia, but she would just brush it off. He always did. Everyone thought nothing of it and would just make jokes and laugh about it.

As the night progressed, he began to be more aggressive with the more alcohol he consumed.

At one point, he cornered Mia in the kitchen when she went to refill her drink. He wouldn't let her pass. He told her "I want you. I think you're hot."

Mia replied in her nervous laugh, "get away," and tried to duck under his arms that had her pinned in between the corner of the kitchen cabinets.

He stood just over six foot tall with a solid frame. Mia was petite and five foot six inches.

He grabbed her by her arms and placed her back in the corner.

"Where do you think you're going? You're not going to get away from me." He said, looking her in her eyes in his firm, drunken voice.

She looked back at the darkness in his eyes, "let me go!" Her voice got louder, and he released his arms and let her go.

Mia tried to leave the kitchen to get away from him, but he grabbed her arms again. This time, from behind.

As she looked around, all the sudden, the entire house became silent. Everyone seemed to have randomly disappeared within minutes.

"I'm not done with you." She heard him say insistently.

She forcefully pulled her arm away from his grip.

He grabbed hold of her again.This time, pushing her from behind and forcing her into the living room couch. He threw her on her back and climbed on top, pinning her arms once again to the couch.

"Get away from me!" She yelled and tried to release his grip.

Nobody was around.

He laughed at her as if her words didn't matter. He moved her arms to pin them above her head with one hand, and the other hand tried to take off her pants.

Tears silently fell down her cheek as she knew what he was trying to do. She fought his hold and wiggled her hips to escape.

He laughed and grabbed her legs again, this time he threw them upwards and placed them over his shoulder. He gripped the top of her pants and pulled harder. He became somewhat successful, as he was able to take them down a few inches.

She tried kicking him.

Nothing affected him and the adrenaline rushing through his veins.

"Stop touching me!" She yelled and the tears started flooding her vision.

He heard nothing. Nor did anyone else.

She thought *where the fuck is everyone? Why is no one hearing me yell? Where did they all go? Why is this happening? And all in the open, and no one is here to save me!* Everyone seemed to have vanished out of thin air.

He pulled one last time, and in one more movement had her pants and underwear around her lower legs, which must have given him some kind of leverage and he forced his fingers inside of her.

"I know you want this." He said and he felt a pleasure of feeling her.

She tried to throw her hips up to gain momentum to release him and kicked him, but he just used her momentum to place her in a tighter ball. She felt his head go down on her.

She kept yelling and begging for him to stop.

Still no sight or sound from anyone around.

She started punching him, but he just fought her defensive movements as if they were nothing. Like he had no feelings.

While he continued to please himself, she fought him with everyone ounce of any energy she had. At one

 point, she knew she had completely disconnected herself from what was happening.

When it was all over, he got up and said, "I'm going to have a smoke." She watched him walk out the front door and shakingly put her clothes back on her half-naked body.

She was in shock.

In disbelief as to what happened.

As the front door closed, she walked into the front hallway where she saw her friend standing at the top of her stairs looking over the banister.

"Where were you? I've been waiting for you. I was getting high in my room. Wanna join me?" Her friend asked without a single knowing of what her boyfriend just did.

"Would love to," Mia replied.

She went into her friend's room and smoked a big joint with her, trying to numb herself from what she had just experienced.

Mia never mentioned a word to her friend or anyone else for that matter. Scared nobody would believe her. All she wanted was to pretend in her mind that that it never happened. To bury it deep inside of her, forever.

From that moment on, Mia's addictions escalated, and she became completely dependent on functioning each day with them.

A functioning stoner by day and a blackout alcoholic by night.

Mia started to put on weight and noticed the guys becoming less interested in her. *A perfect means of protection* she thought. And within a few months, she found herself weighing just over two hundred pounds.

She stopped caring for herself. She didn't see the point anymore. She felt people either didn't care or would only hurt her.

All she wanted was to not feel pain anymore. Not from anyone or anything.

This cycle continued for about a year until her gallbladder stopped working and she was forced to lose weight and get sobered up for her surgery.

That's when she put herself into therapy.

As she worked on herself and her healing, she also recognized her spiritual gifts started to come back. To reawaken. Another part of herself she had buried as a child because her sister had always told her she was crazy whenever Mia shared her premonitions with her. Mia believed her.

As the year passed and the more Mia focused on herself and her healing, the more she started to tune into who she really was, to learn to love herself, and find her worth from within.

Chapter Fourteen

Another week passed and Mia was now comfortable with Adam not being part of her new life. She was feeling better than ever about where she was on her journey, everything she had overcome so far, and embracing all of who she was.

The more she worked on herself, she knew certain relationships had to end so she could make space for new beginnings. Her heart now understood how and why each person had come into her life, and for which purpose they served her. To help her heal from her sacred scars.

She worked on releasing what she had outgrown and the person she once was. And even made peace in her heart with the people that were once part of her old life.

Although challenging to let go of those she loved so dearly, she knew that if she held on to the time when those old relationships began, she would have kept herself from expanding into her greatest version of who she is.

The music played on her dryer letting her know her load of laundry was now finished.

She went into her bedroom and grabbed her hamper and took out the clothes.

She walked back and dumped the pile of warm lavender-scented clothes onto her bed.

She must have dropped her phone somewhere under the pile of clean clothes as she heard her phone faintly ding that she had received a new text message.

She dug her way through the warmth and heard it chime a second time, helping her locate exactly where it fell.

As she pulled it out of the pile, she saw she received a text message. It was from Adam.

Hi, beautiful. I miss you so much. I haven't stopped thinking about you. I can't get you off my mind. I had to message you. How are you? How is everything with your separation going? Hope everything is still going well. Still happy with your decision?

Mia stood there just staring at his message. She could feel that he sincerely missed her.

She placed her phone back on her bed and grabbed another piece of laundry to fold.

Her gut had been telling her that she would be hearing from him soon. She somehow felt that pull in her energy from him getting stronger again the last couple of days.

She was feeling strong and was proud of the inner strength she gained over these past weeks in his absence. She didn't want to reply right away. She wanted some time to reflect on how she felt, even though a part of her was happy he texted. That he wasn't a complete asshole.

She put her final piece of folded shirts away and closed her drawer.

The sun was shining through her bedroom window with the early spring. She wanted to take advantage of this beautiful weather and knew that going for a walk always brought her clarity.

Mia put on a light grey zip-up sweater over her white t-shirt, slipped her feet into her light pink running shoes, and stepped out her front door.

Maybe, this little time apart helped him realize his true feelings for her, she thought.

She took a deep cleansing breath.

She knew in her heart, although this last while was heartbreaking, Mia was also grateful for this time away from him. It gave her the time to work on herself and explore some old parts of herself that needed to be healed.

She strolled around her neighbourhood and noticed all the tulips that were beginning to bloom. She loved the feeling of springtime as it always felt like a period of rebirth and renewal.

She got back to her house and sat on her couch with a cup of
matcha tea. She looked at her phone, took another deep breath, and began to type her reply.

I am doing well and keeping busy. How are you?
Yes, still happy with my decision. Hope you are well.

As soon as she pressed send, she could see the three dots moving across the bottom of the screen with
his next message popping upwards.

I want you back. I am sorry I did what I did. I was just so scared. You were just coming out of a huge marriage, and I didn't want to be the rebound. I wouldn't be able to live with myself if I was a reason, you didn't get back with her former husband.

She had no idea that he felt or even thought of it that way. Mia typed back.

I decided to leave because I had been unhappy with him for many years. It had nothing to do with you. You coming into my life was a blessing. You helped me discover so many new things about myself. I am forever very grateful.

There was a pause between their messages.

I am no longer seeing that other person. I ended it because I couldn't get you off my mind. It didn't feel right. So many thoughts going through my mind. I hope that we could plan another visit soon.

She took another minute before she responded. Let me think about this and look at my schedule.

My schedule is busy with work the upcoming weeks, but I have a couple of days off after that? I would love to try this out with you again. He wrote back.

I will confirm with you tomorrow. Enjoy the rest of your day. Xo. Mia told Adam.

You too babe. Xoxo. Was his final reply for that day.

She took a deep breath and called her friend.

She told her what had just happened and that she thought about giving this all another try. Mia explained that she understood his fears. There were so many moving pieces to their relationship that she could comprehend his apprehension.

The complexities of him living in a different country, where he had built his life and his successful career. She was now focused on rebuilding her own life, with all her latest changes.

She told her friend, if they are meant to be together, then it will happen. In the meantime, she will continue to focus on herself and go with the flow.

Plus, she wasn't dating anyone else. She became very particular with whom she wanted to date and wasn't having much luck. Adam seemed to keep fitting what she desired. Another chance is what she would probably give him.

She wanted to sleep on it first she told her friend and would let her know her final decision in the morning.

Chapter Fifteen

She woke up to her alarm.

5:00 am

She had barely slept because she was contemplating her decision to go to see him again or not.

Mia couldn't disregard the feelings she felt since his messages. She felt the reignition of their magnetic pull towards each other getting stronger overnight and noticed it had fizzled out and completely disappeared when she felt his absence.

Since his most recent texts, the pull was becoming hard to ignore. This urge, this tugging sensation for him that she questioned all night.

She struggled to get out of bed from her restless night, but she had an early start at work and had to be out of the house before rush-hour traffic began.

She hopped and of bed and quickly got ready and jumped in her car and put it into drive.

The sun was rising along the horizon with the most beautiful hues of pink and orange.

It reminded her of the sunrise and sunsets in Colorado. Mia interpreted this as a sign of confirmation for her to give their relationship another try.

The traffic moved well, and she even got to work a little earlier than usual.

She had a quick morning meeting with her boss and was grateful that she was up to date with all her work. This would allow her to check in with Adam today and confirm their plans.

It would still be a few hours until he would be up, so she got to work right away in hopes she could leave early.

After getting her first assignment completed and some emails sent, she went to have a quick coffee break.

She looked in her purse to see if she still had a gift card for the local café and noticed her phone glow.

Three missed text messages from Adam.

She had forgotten it was still on vibrate.

She thought it was odd that he was up so early. *Perhaps he had a sleepless night too?*

Morning beautiful. Was the first text.

I couldn't sleep last night thinking that I might not see you again. Was the second message she read, followed by his third text, **I miss you. I adore you. Xo.**

She felt a smile appear on her face.

I miss you too. Checking for flights later today. Will confirm after work and pressed send.

She felt excited at the thought of seeing him again soon. To feel his arms wrapped around her and his lip pressed against hers.

She left her office and walked across the street to purchase her usual coffee with almond milk.

She quickly made her way back to her office with excitement so she can check for flights before getting back to work.

The departure flight would arrive around eleven in the morning and return at one o'clock in the afternoon on the third day. This would be perfect. Enough time to see each other during those few days.

Mia only had a few more emails to write and send off then was able to sneak early from work. It was hard for her to focus on her work from her lack of sleep, combined with her excitement to see him again.

After her last email was sent, Mia checked in with her boss before calling it a day.

"Nothing else for today, Mia. Thank you and enjoy the rest of your night." Her boss told her.

"Thank you, you as well," Mia replied and took her keys out of
her coat pocket and headed towards the parking lot.

She got in her car and decided to surprise Adam and call him on her drive home.

The phone rang and went straight to his voicemail. She didn't leave a message. She knew he would see her missed call.

She put on the radio and got lost in whatever songs they played.

It all seemed so synchronistic. The songs that played on the radio reminded her of him. All the signs were once again pointing towards him.

Her drive home was smooth as she had missed all the crazy traffic. As she was about to pull into her driveway, her music was interrupted by Adam calling her back.

"Hello," Mia said.

"Hey, babe. Sorry, I was on another call. There's a temporary contract job in New York that I might get. I will start next month. Just trying to work out the details." Adam informed her.

"Oh, that's great news. Congratulations! Wishing you all the best." She replied.

"So, did you figure out those dates? Can you make them work to come and see me?" He asked.

"They do!" She said with excitement. "I will send you the flight details and pickup times shortly. I just pulled into my driveway from work. I'm happy to hear your voice though. It's been so long."

"Sounds great. On those dates I gave you, I am off and pretty flexible with time. I just might have to do a couple of things to prepare for this job when you are here. I hope you don't mind. It's a good opportunity for me but miss you so much and I would love to see you too before I go."

"I understand. As long as I can see you for a few days and be in your arms again, that's all I want." She told him.

"Me too, babe."

"Ok, I am just getting into my house. I will send the details in a few minutes. Touch base soon, ok."

"Can't wait. Talk soon. Mwah." She heard him say on the other end of the phone.

"Bye, handsome." She said with a huge smile on her face.

She unlocked her front door and stepped inside while opening the travel app to send him the flight details.

He texted her back right away. **Works perfect, babe. Book it!**

Moments later she had booked her tickets.

She was so excited she went right to her room to see what clothes she would pack this time.

She searched through her hangers and already knew what different outfits she would bring. All she had to do now was go out and buy herself at least one new set of lingerie and she would be ready to go.

Chapter Sixteen

2:35 am

Her alarm woke her. She had to be at the airport for her 6:05 am flight.

All her bags were packed and ready to go. All she needed to do was take a quick shower and put on her clothes. She laid them out the night before and would apply her makeup right before they landed. She wanted to get as much rest as she could prior to her departure as she knew she wouldn't be getting much sleep over the next three days.

They had spent the last two weeks talking and laughing over the phone, and multiple texts messages back and forth. She felt good about where the direction of their relationship was going and the nudges of the universe pulling them closer towards each other every day.

She finished getting ready, grabbed her belongings, locked her front door, and placed her bags in her trunk.

It was still dark out when she left for the airport. This time, she wasn't as nervous about travelling alone.

She arrived at her terminal and was pleased to find a parking spot close to the bridge that was directly across from her airline.

The airport appeared to be busier than her last travel experience even though it was still really early in the morning.

The lineups were a lot longer than the previous time and people around her were already impatient, which started to give her some anxiety.

After about thirty minutes in line, she finally got her boarding pass and made her way over to the US customs line, which seemed to have now tripled since she had arrived.

It looked chaotic and unorganized. Passengers started to push their way in front of the lines, so they didn't miss their flights.

Mia hadn't moved an inch in over twenty minutes and her nerves started to get the better of her. She was beginning to worry too, that she might miss her flight.

She heard the customs worker call out flight numbers. For those passengers to come forward to bypass the line so they didn't miss their flight. She was one of them.

People pushed trying to hear and make their way to the front of the line. Mia had never seen anything like this before.

She finally got to the front of the line and showed her flight details to the customs attendant. She let Mia pass towards the customs officers and was quickly cleared.

From then on, it was a race to her gate. She made it with five minutes to spare before her boarding time.

5:16am

Mia was frazzled and sweating from all the rushing and adrenaline running through her body.

She got in line to board her plane and was relieved when she finally sat in her seat beside the window. This time, she was seating over the wing of the plane. She didn't care. As long as she was beside a window to catch some glimpses of the spectacular aerial views.

She took out her phone before takeoff and texted

Adam that her flight was on time, and she couldn't wait to kiss his soft and sexy lips.

She settled in the plane with a sigh of relief. She was well on her way. She felt the fatigue creep in her body from her early start and all the stress she experienced in the airport over the last three hours.

Mia reached under the seat in front of her and grabbed her neck pillow and placed it between her and the window where she laid her head to rest.

She looked out the window and felt the swaying back and forth motions of the aircraft as it made its way down the runway for takeoff.

Minutes after the plane reached its altitude, she felt the heaviness of her eye close, and she drifted off to sleep.

Chapter Seventeen

She suddenly awoke from the shaking of the plane from a mild turbulence followed with the announcement form the pilot's voice making sure that all passengers remain seated and put on their seatbelts.

She looked out the window and saw that they were flying over grey rainclouds with mountain peaks peeking through. *We must be close to landing,* she thought.

She looked at the screen in front of her of the digital map of the image of their airplane traveling. They were close to their arrival.

She watched through the window their descent through the stormy clouds and how the rain fell on the plane's exterior.

The pilot made another announcement to instruct everyone to prepare for landing and that they would be arriving in about fifteen minutes.

Mia reattached her neck pillow on the handle of her oversized purse that was under the seat in front of her and took out her makeup bag to quickly apply it on her face before landing.

She felt the butterflies reappear in her stomach when she saw they were about to land. She could already feel the embrace of the arms of her lover once more.

11:57 am

The rain had stopped by the time she got through the airport. She made her way over to her pickup spot where she arrived just on time to see his black Lexus SUV pulling up towards her.

She beamed when she saw his sexy smile framed with his scruffy beard drive up right in front of her.

He walked around the front of his vehicle and firmly grabbed her by her waist to pull her in for a kiss.

"God, you look even more beautiful this time. Is that even possible?" He said and kissed her again.

"I am happy to see you too, sexy." Mia replied and kissed him back.

She felt his soft nibble on her bottom lip and squeezed her harder.

"Let's get outta here. I can't wait to get you home." He said in a hurry and grabbed her luggage and quickly placed it in his trunk.

They both got in the car and drove off.
She felt his hand firmly touch her upper thigh. "Oh my god, babe, you're so hot!" He said under his breath, and she felt his hand move further up to her inner thigh.

"I missed you." Mia whispered back and grabbed his upper thigh and slowly moved her hand upwards.

He slammed on his breaks as he almost hit the car that was now only inches in front of them.

"Ok, we better stop so I can concentrate on my driving so I can get us home safely." He said with his eyes wide open and in a slightly disappointed tone.

He removed his hand from her thigh and took hers from his and gave her hand a kiss.

"No more teasing right now." He said.

She missed his kisses. He was always kissing her and wanting to hold her when they were together. Something she missed. The physical touch. Something that had drifted apart in her marriage.

"It's even more beautiful this time of year with everything beginning to bloom here." She observed on their drive back to his place.

She could see all the fresh buds the flowers and the lush hues of greens on the trees starting to fill out.

He turned right onto the road that led up the mountain towards his house. It felt like it was only yesterday she had pulled into his driveway for the first time.

As soon as he parked, he unbuckled his seatbelt and placed one hand on her thigh and the other hand behind her neck. He firmly pulled him towards her, and she felt his lips and tongue touch hers.

His hand rubbed up and down her thigh.

"I want you." He demanded and unbuckled her seatbelt.

"Me too." She agreed. Her breath getting heavier as she enjoyed feeling his hand running up and down her body.

"Follow me." He said and they both opened their car doors and walked inside his house.

One passionate kiss led to the next as they made their way towards his bedroom, leaving behind a trail of their clothes.

He threw her down on his bed as she laid with her legs spread open, inviting him in for more. He got on top of her fully naked body and paused for a brief moment. He gazed deep into her eyes and without saying a word, inserted himself inside her.

Chapter Eighteen

2:12 pm

Their tired naked bodies lied intertwined with each other as Adam drifted off to sleep. It had been an early day for both of them and they both felt exhausted from the anticipation of their reunion.

Mia closed her eyes and simply enjoyed the sensation of his body around hers along with the sound of his breathing while he slept.

She was finally happy. The last month speaking with him in their long-distance relationship had led them to this very moment.

That pull that had catapulted her into this relationship seemed to dissipate each time they got together. It felt as though their souls aligned with each other from the fragmented pieces when they were apart.

Her body began to get too hot with his around hers. She didn't want to wake him and tried to quietly move, but he must have felt her. He lifted his head and opened his eyes. He glanced at her then released his hold.

"Sorry, babe, I am getting so hot." Mia told him.

He kissed her forehead. "Let me just sleep a little bit longer. But please, stay here. You feel good next to me." And he turned the other way and quickly dozed off to sleep.

She closed her eyes in hopes that she would fall asleep and have a little rest too, but she just wanted to enjoy this moment. With him. His body. His touch. With him next to her.

4:04 pm

"I feel nice and rested." She heard him say when he woke up and turned his body toward hers. "How about you?"

"Rested and starving!" Mia replied. "What do you feel like doing for dinner?" She asked.

"I was thinking of taking you to this cute little village where they have a bunch of restaurants. My favourites are the Mexican one or the Japanese restaurant. What do you feel like eating?"

"Why don't we try the Japanese one. We ate Mexican last time I was here. Try something new? Sounds good?" She suggested.

"I am good with either. Let's go get ready and leave in say, in an hour?" He asked.

"I can be ready in an hour." She confirmed.

He spanked her bare ass as she got out of bed, then walked down the hall to the spare bathroom to turn on the shower.

She noticed Adam had neatly laid out a couple of towels for her on the counter. He always tried to make her feel comfortable in his home.

She turned the shower off then grabbed one of the nicely folded towels to dry her body. She wasn't sure how long she was but felt a little less rushed when she could hear his shower still running in his bathroom. Still, she hated being late and wanted to make sure she was within the sixty-minute time frame.

All she needed to do was re-apply her makeup and she already knew what outfit she was going to wear. Her faux leather pants with her see-through black blouse and her black stiletto heels.

Just as she finished getting ready, Adam called out to her to see if she was almost ready.

"Another two minutes and I'll be good to go." She told him.

"Great! I love how punctual you are. Meet me downstairs by the garage doors. I'll be putting my shoes on."

Mia put on her black fitted coat and placed the handle for her clutch purse around her wrist and made her way to meet Adam. He was just about to open the door to the garage when he saw her approaching.

"Babe, you look so hot!" He told her again. Something she loved to hear him say.

"Thanks!" She said back and grabbed his face to kiss him. "Just wait 'til we get back from dinner. I was thinking we could have each other for dessert?" She said as she looked at him and lightly bit her bottom lip with anticipation.

"Fuck, you're hot!" Adam said as he tried to resist her. She felt his hand smack her ass again as she made her way past him into the garage.

When they pulled out of his driveway, the sun was setting behind the mountains with pink and orange highlights in the sky. She absolutely loved the views here.

She took her left hand and gently placed it behind Adam's neck to give him a light massage as he drove.

He quickly glanced over to Mia and smiled with approval, then quickly turned back to watch the road.

"I really like being here with you." She said to him.

She saw a smile appear on his face. "Me too." He replied and turned on his cellphone to connect his music to his car speakers.

She noticed that whenever she would start to talk about what she felt towards him, he had a hard time expressing his. Instead, he distracted the conversation by playing music.

The songs were always about love. How to fall in love. Think of falling in love. Ways to fall in love. Whatever the mix of songs he played, from the 1960's to present, there was always a reference of love somewhere in there.

There wasn't much traffic on the roads. There never really was there it seemed. Not something to which she was accustomed to. Unlike the many times she had been stuck in the traffic back home. Here, it was open, more spacious. It didn't seem like everyone was in such a rush to commute anywhere. The only major traffic she had experienced there so far was about five cars stopped in front of them at a stop light.

She released her hand from the back of his neck and took his hand to kiss his soft hand.

He turned into a large plaza on the left. Mia saw different kinds of clothing stores, a grocery store, and some restaurants that were tucked away in a little courtyard in the back with strands of lights, lighting up the path along the brick walkway.

They each got out of the car and Mia felt the wind had picked up from earlier. He walked towards her to interlock his fingers with hers and made their way down the lit path toward the restaurant.

They passed by the Mexican restaurant he mentioned. It did look intriguing, but it seemed like whenever they did get together, all the ate were nachos and guacamole. She felt it was time to try something new together.

They arrived at the Japanese place, and he opened the restaurant door. She felt him place his hand on her low back to gently guide her first into the entranceway where they were immediately greeted by the hostess.

"Welcome. For two?" She asked and took two menus.

"Yes. Can we please get a booth?" He asked.
"I have one ready for you. Right this way." She replied and walked to the left of the restaurant.

She placed the menus on the table. Mia sat down and to her surprise, Adam sat right next to her in the booth.

"I want to be close to you." He said looking at Mia and picked up his menu.

"Can I get you any drinks? Sake?"

"I've actually never tried Sake before." Mia ashamedly admitted.

"Well, Sake it is then!" Adam said to the waiter.

"I can't believe you have never had sake before! You'll like it!" He said as she felt his hand rub up her thigh and kissed her on the side of her neck.

The server returned moments later with two little porcelain cups and a bottle of Sake.

He was right. She did enjoy the Sake. They even ordered a second bottle before finishing dinner. The entire time, he couldn't keep his hands off her. Rubbing his hand along her thighs and low back.

"I'm thinking we head back to my place and watch some movies tonight. A nice relaxing night." He suggested as the server come with their bill.

"Yes. I am totally in the mood to curl up in front of the TV with you." She told him.

He finished paying the bill and walked her back to his car and opened the passenger side door for her to get in.

"Thank you." She said to him as she sat down.

She watched him walk around the front of the car and open his door to get in.

He looked at Mia and smiled and put his keys in the ignition and started his car.

He reached over to hold her hand once more and off they drove.

9:18 pm

Was the time she saw on microwave when they walked into his kitchen.

"I am feeling really tired today. I was hoping you don't mind we get our pj's on and just watch a movie in the bedroom?" He asked.

"I am easy going. Whatever you're up for." She answered.

Mia went to the spare room to put on her soft pink silky negligee then crawled into Adam's bed where he was already lying in a black t-shirt and navy-blue boxers.

"Come here." He said with an outstretched arm and gestured her to cuddle alongside of him. She felt the warmth of his body against hers as she rested her head on his slightly hairy chest and wrapped her top leg around his.

He pulled the blankets over top of her to keep her warm. "There. All comfy?" He asked her and kissed her forehead.

"Yes. Thank you." She replied and wrapped her arm around his chest, then pressed play on his favourite drama movie he had been wanting to watch with Mia.

Chapter Nineteen

Mia woke in complete darkness. They had both fallen asleep in each other's arms while watching the movie.

5:54 am

It had been so long since she had such a restful night's sleep and she felt energized, and at peace.

Adam was still sound asleep. It was too early to make any movements that she decided to continue to lay quietly beside him.

She liked the presence of him sleeping beside her. She was still not completely used to sleeping all alone, even though she had a hard time with someone sleeping next to her.

7:12 am

Adam must have woken to the rays of daylight shining on him in bed as the sun came through the window. He turned and pulled Mia close to his body and kissed her softly on her lips.

"Morning." He said in his raspy sexy morning voice. "You fell asleep in my arms last night. I didn't want to wake you. You looked so peaceful." He told her.

Mia took a deep breath. He felt what she felt. A sense of peace.

"I did feel peaceful in your arms last night." She agreed and took another breath to feel her body sink deeper into his.

He looked at her and softly ran his fingers along her face.

"You look so beautiful." He whispered softly.

"Are you sure?" She laughed in disbelief. "I have no makeup on, and I probably have bad morning breath." She said trying to cover her mouth when she spoke.

"You are. And no, you don't." He said to her and kissed her again.

"I have to get some work done this morning. I'm gonna go make some coffee and get started so we can have the later half of the day to ourselves." He gave her one more kiss before getting out of bed to get the day started.

She got her workout clothes on and met him downstairs for a quick morning coffee. On her last visit, she had established a spot on the area rug in front of the sliding doors where she sipped her coffee and pulled some tarot cards.

His spot was in a medium brown winged back leather chair that had a matching ottoman where he rested his feet. She would secretly watch him from the corner of her eyes. Observing him sipping on his coffee while scrolling through his emails and text messages.

At times he would even laugh out loud at whatever he was reading. Mia would just look and him and wonder what he was laughing at. He didn't share too many details with her. He liked to be mysterious, she thought.

"Would you like me to pour you another coffee before I head into my office?" Adam asked Mia.

"I would love another one, please." He walked over to take her cup and refill it.

"There you go babe." As he gave her cup back. "Make yourself at home. I should be a few hours." He said and she watched him walk down the hall and into his office.

She shuffled her tarot deck one more time and *The Hermit* card flew out of the deck and onto the floor.

The Hermit meaning suggests a journey inward of reflection and meditation to discover any answers you seek, that you will only find in your solitude. A pathway to discover your inner wisdom and knowing.

How fitting she thought. She had been standing on unsteady ground for the last several months and felt as though she had been uprooted once more with all her inner questions, contemplating her next step.

She put the cards away and went to the kitchen sink to wash their cups.

She didn't mind that Adam had work to do. It was a way to experience real life scenarios with him while she was there visiting.

She wanted to go on a run, but she wasn't used to the altitude there. She tried to run outdoors the last time she was there, and it took her three days before she could run for even twenty minutes. She decided to run on his treadmill in his workout room instead that was in his basement, away from his office. At least this way, she wasn't afraid of making too much noise that might distract him from his work.

10:52 am

Was the time she finished her workout. She went right to the shower so she could be ready for whenever he finished whatever work he was working on.

As she dried herself off, she was a little startled to hear there was a knock on the bathroom door.

"Can I come in?" She heard him say on the other side of the door.

She was still naked and quickly wrapped the towel around her. *Not like this,* she thought to herself. Her hair was soaking wet, and she didn't like to be seen without makeup on. She slowly opened the door a crack.

"Sorry, is there something you need?" she asked slightly confused.

"You." He said and he finished opening the door and pulled her towards him.

Her towel immediately fell to the ground. She felt his hand reach around and grab her ass. She felt him squeeze it hard while his other hand gently grabbed the back of her head to pull her in towards his lips. They stumbled down the hall towards his bedroom.

He turned her around. Her back against his torso. She felt him kiss the side of her neck while sliding his hands down the front of her body.

He bent her forward over his bed. Her feet flat on the floor. She felt him grab her hips and pull her into him and his deep thrusting motion inside of her.

They both moaned with pleasure.

She felt him kiss her between her shoulder blades after he came.

"Mmmm." He moaned again.

"I have few more things to finish with work." He said to her surprise.

"I thought you were done your work?" She asked in a confused tone.

"I didn't want your sexy naked body to go to waste. I won't be long. Twenty minutes. Enough time for you to finish getting ready." He told her as he zipped up his pants and made his way back toward his office.

11:32 am

After getting ready, Mia walked down the hall towards the living room and saw Adam standing there. He looked up and saw her walking down the stairs.

"Perfect timing. Let's get our shoes on and head out for the day." He suggested.

One full day to spend with him and she wanted to make the most of it. It didn't matter what he needed to do, as long as she was with him, that was all that mattered to her.

They drove around all day getting last-minute things he needed for work and even went to his favourite record store.

7:02 pm

They went back to the house. Adam had suggested he make frozen pizzas and sip on wine for dinner.

They laughed and shared more stories while eating their pizzas in his kitchen.

He poured a third glass of wine for the two of them when they were full and suggested they move over to the couch to be more comfortable.

Before sitting down, Mia excused herself and handed her glass of wine to Adam.

She walked into the bedroom where she kept her clothes and opened her suitcase to put on something a little sexier. She pulled out her black lace corset lingerie piece, her knee-high pantyhose and slipped on her black stilettos.

As she got closer to the top of the stairs, she saw Adam scrolling on his phone.

When she placed her right foot on the top stair, Adam noticed her coming down the staircase. He looked. His eyes opened wide.

"Holy shit." He said with excitement and sat in complete stillness as he watched her walk over to him.

Mia took his wine glass from his hand and placed it on the table beside them.

She felt him grab her waist and pull her onto his lap. Their eyes locked as her hips began to move up and down on top of him, feeling him getting harder underneath her with each movement.

His hands moved along her legs and thighs begging her for more.

He tried to kiss her, but she smirked and pulled away. Teasing him even more.

She kissed his neck and slowly made her way down his torso to undue his pants.

He moaned and pulled her back up as she licked his hard shaft, taunting him until he couldn't take it anymore.

She lifted her head and licked him all the back up towards his neck before moving him inside of her.

He looked into her eye and moaned in ecstasy.

Chapter Twenty

8:00 am

Mia's alarm was going off. They only had a couple of hours of sleep as they made love to each other all night.

"Morning Adam," she said and kissed his shoulder. "I know it's early, but I have to get up and get going."

"I'll get up. Just give me a few more minutes." He said and rolled the other way.

"I'm going to finish packing. I'll come wake you when I am done." And left the bedroom to get dressed and ready to go.

9:42 am

Mia crawled back into bed beside him and gave him another kiss on his shoulder.

"Time to get up." She spoke softly.

He rolled back towards her and hugged her.

"I'm really going to miss you this time." He said and kissed her softly on her lips.

"Me too. But I really don't want to be late. We have to get going now. Please." Mia told him again. She hated being late for anything and never liked feeling rushed. It always gave her too much anxiety.

"I'll be ready in five minutes." He responded.

"I'll bring my bags downstairs. We'll have just enough time for a quick coffee." She said. She always needed her morning coffee and so did he.

10: 07 am

They packed all her bags in the trunk and drove off towards the airport.

"Maybe you can come visit me when I go to New York? I will be there for a few months. I will look at my schedule and see when I have a three-day weekend. I could show you another new part of the world." He said optimistically.

"That would be amazing!" Mia replied with a smile of hope.

He pulled up to the curb outside of the departure zone and they both got out of his car.

"I am so happy I got to see you. That you gave me another chance." He said while holding her tight against his body. His sensual kisses gave her butterflies.

"Me too." She answered back.

"I'll message you when I land." She said and gave him one last kiss then turned to enter the airport.

She looked back at him when she stepped inside, and they each blew each other one last kiss.

Mia made her way to her gate without any run-ins this time. Without the chaos of passengers pushing their way through lines and without any guns.

It was a peaceful flight and drive home.

11:43 pm

Mia texted Adam to let him know she was home safely. He replied right away letting her know he was happy to hear she arrived.

As you know, I'm going to be extra busy the next few days leading up to my departure. Getting everything ready for work and packing and all. I will touch base as soon as I can. Good night. Sweet dreams. And ended his text with a kissy-face emoji.

Mia was exhausted from her whirlwind of travel and the little sleep she had over the past three days. She had to be up early again the next morning to go back to her office and was eager to get some shuteye.

She got into her pajamas, plopped herself into bed, and quickly fell fast asleep.

Chapter Twenty-One

It had already been a week since Mia had come back and still no text from Adam. She knew he had a lot on his plate but still hoped that he would have at least checked in with her at some point.

She did think about him every day and was trying to make sense of their temporary magnetism between them like an on and off switch.

She felt it. Every time this pulling force gained strength, she felt him coming back to her life and then it would completely disappear with his absence.

She had never felt this so intensely with anyone else before. Only with him.

It was like he would crave Mia and when he felt satiated by her, he moved towards a new craving.

This yo-yo feeling left her confused and heartbroken. She had been through so many losses with people throughout her life. People she loved and cared for; it was starting to take a toll on her.

She remembered *The Hermit* card from the tarot deck she pulled the last day she was with Adam. It gave her insight of what was to come.

It all started to make sense now.

But still, she wanted to make sure he was ok. She picked up her phone and began to type.

Hi Adam. I just wanted to check in with you to see how you are doing. Hope all is well? Xo.

6:05 pm

She placed her phone on her kitchen counter to prepare something to eat. She was starving. She had now regained some of her appetite she had lost over the last few days thinking about this pattern with Adam.

She didn't keep much in her fridge since she lived alone and couldn't remember what food she even had stored. Mia opened the refrigerator to see what was inside.

A carton of coconut milk, some fruit, olives, and spinach. She looked on her counter and saw a ripe banana.

A banana shake it is she thought.

She grabbed her milk, banana, some frozen peaches from her freezer, vanilla protein powder, and a pinch of cinnamon, ginger, and turmeric. It was her favourite go to meal.

She put all the ingredients into a blender to mix, then poured it into a cup and put a straw in it.

She walked into her living room and sat on the couch and started scrolling through social media.

She wasn't posting too many things these days. Her former husband would make comments to her regarding how he would follow her every move on social media, what posts she was liking, or not liking. Mia couldn't be bothered with all that drama. So, she did nothing for the time being other than read inspirational quotes.

7:18 pm

She heard her phone with a notification.

It was from Adam. **You've been on my mind. How's it going?**

She wasn't sure how to respond as he didn't acknowledge or answer anything she asked. Did he not see what she wrote?

I'm good. She typed back. **Hope you are enjoying NY. Xo.**

Mia felt sad.

She knew in her heart she had made the right decision months ago to leave her married life. That old image of who she was no longer existed but had no idea that she would face so many ups and downs in the process.

She couldn't contain her tears any longer.

That's it, she thought. *This shit again? Why does it feel so hard to feel loved?*

All she ever longed for was to receive the love that she gave to those around her. To feel happy with. To laugh with. To explore the world and go on adventures with, and to share that life with someone.

Mia felt the division of her opposing emotions of feeling lost and scared one moment, versus her gut telling her she was on the right path. But it was hard for her to clearly see at times with all the destruction occurring around her and her relationships.

She would pray every day and night for clarity, strength, and guidance. That each step she took, her path was illuminated.

For now, she needed to sit with the pain that could no longer be ignored.

Her tears fell down her face like a rainstorm and soaked the decorative pillow like a puddle.

She was tired of holding it all in. Tired of trying to hold it all together and shoving the truth from the hurtful wounds of betrayal aside.

9:18 pm

Her head hurt from all her crying, but she felt a huge release in her heart.

She got up from the remnants of her tears and took a deep breath. She stood to walk towards the kitchen to take something for her headache.

She wanted to take a bath but felt too physically and emotionally exhausted. Instead, she put on her pajamas and tucked herself into bed.

Chapter Twenty-Two

6:15 am

The hot sun was already peeking through her window on this mid-summer morning when she heard the music on her phone letting her know it was time to get up and get ready for her run.

Over the last few months, she had heard from Adam periodically with his occasional check-ins.

The push and pull with his energy was too overwhelming for Mia. She kept cutting energetic cords with him, but he would always come back telling her how much his missed her but would never follow through on any future plans to see each other again.

When her emotions become too shattering from all the changes and challenges, she faced, she had turned to drinking and drugs for a brief period of time. Her pain had become too unbearable, but she did not want to go backwards down that rabbit hole of old pattern of self-destructive behaviours. Instead, she turned her focus to long distance running and used that method as her therapy.

Mia dedicated her mornings to meditation to go deeper within where she tuned into her heart and asked herself what it was, she needed to give in that moment. Love? Peace? Feelings of gratitude for her strength and courage?

She would then get dressed in her workout clothes, tie up her running shoes and head out the door and run for hours.

She never listened to music while running. She used her runs to release any emotions she felt she needed to and felt grounded and calm when she connected with mother nature. This became her way of being.

It was a quiet Saturday morning when Mia realized she began to love her solitude. She no longer felt alone. Instead, she felt inner peace.

Over these past few months, she had poured so much love and focused on herself. Something she had never done before.

She felt herself shift. She became stronger and empowered with the choices she had made.

These last months in Hermit mode, she recognized that everyone that had left her during the past little while, they were all her muses of inspiration. They left her life for a reason. Not because they abandoned her, but because she had outgrown them by who she was becoming. Who she was always meant to be.

All her phases of expansion and contractions throughout her life, launched her further into her growth.

Today, she stood the strongest she had ever been before.

And the more Mia truly learned to love herself, she began to develop new friendship that felt deep and real to her. The connections she had been seeking in relationships.

These new friends felt like soul sisters to her. No judgements or insults. They were just like her. Wanting the same outcomes in relationships. To be loved, honoured, heard, understood, and supported with whatever decisions were being made. Because whatever the case was, it didn't matter, these friendships that blossomed were about building each other up to the best of their abilities. To achieve their greatest potential.

7:51 am

The drenched clothes from her sweat went right to wash after her run. Mia turned on a hot shower. Even though it was summer. She loved hot showers.

She was filled with excitement for later that night. She was meeting a new friend she met from work to attend her first boat party.

After her shower, she got dressed and left her house to finish a few errands she wanted to complete as early as possible.

On her way home from her errands, she stopped by one of her favourite stores to see if she could find anything else that would capture her eye to wear for the night. She wanted to look exceptionally good because she felt so good about herself and wanted to feel good in her outfit, especially because she hadn't been out dancing for years.

Unfortunately, she didn't find anything, but since it was such a beautiful day, she wasn't quite ready to head home. She wanted to stay outside a little longer and enjoy the weather.

Mia drove back to her house to park her car and went for a walk around her neighborhood park where she was getting quite familiar with a lot of people in her community. She always saw the same friendly faces and even started having small conversations with some of the people as they walked around.

She loved to stroll around a nearby path at her local park and always enjoyed hearing the laughter from the children playing.

"How ya doing?" Mia heard a familiar voice.

She had seen this mother before walking around the path getting her exercise in too and she always said hello to Mia.

Mia smiled and replied "I'm good thank you. You?"

"Good thanks! Have a great day!" She replied in her cheery voice and they both kept walking past each other.

Mia's heart was feeling full of joy as she took in all her surroundings and the hot warm sun that was shining down on her face.

Her phone buzzed.

She looked down and it was her friend Natashia letting her know how excited she was about tonight. To meet at 8:30 pm because the boat cruise left at 9:00pm sharp.

Mia confirmed she would be there on time. *Another new adventure* she thought. Exactly what she wanted.

3:22 pm

Mia started her walk back toward her house so she could eat a little something and rest for a bit with a cup of coffee before getting ready to go back out.

Her phone buzzed again.

She looked and to her surprise saw it was Adam.

Miss you. Thinking of you.
Part of her still missed him. She knew what a significant role he had played in her life for which she was truly grateful for. He helped her see a new way of being. New possibilities. Helped her have new experiences that she will never forget. Things she would not have seen without him coming into her life. As much as she wanted to be mad at him, she wasn't.

Miss you too she replied and knew she would receive another text in another week or so from him saying the same thing.

The pain wasn't there like it was a little over a month ago. Each day that she focused on her wellbeing, she became more grounded in who she was.

She opened her door to the air-conditioned home and warmed up the leftover coffee from earlier that day. She sat on her couch for a few minutes before heading back to her kitchen to make herself a quick bite to eat.

When it was time to get ready, Mia put on some loud music to dance and sing along to while she did her hair and makeup.
7:21 pm

She texted her friend to let her know she would be leaving shortly as it was an hour-long drive to get to where she was going.

See you soon! Drive safe! Natashia texted back.
Mia pulled up exactly at the same time as Natashia. They even parked beside each other.

They hugged and laughed with excitement and walked towards the deck where the large party boat was docked.

They had arrived right on time. The music played loudly over the speakers while they made their way toward the bow of the boat and found their spot where they would hang out at the rest of the night and dance.

Before Mia knew it, the boat was full of partyers, and the captain announced it was time for their departure with a salute of the horn.

Everyone cheered as the boat left its port and the music got even louder. People danced and she felt the floor shake as she took it all in. The more the music played, the further away from shore they got.

Mia had never seen the city views before from this angle. It was absolutely spectacular. All the tall buildings that were lit up alongside the CN Tower, reflected their lights back onto the water like a glass mirror.

Mia had not had that much fun dancing in a long time and was so grateful for this moment. The night seemed to fly by.

1:00 am

The boat had to dock. Natashia and Mia walked back laughing all the way to their cars.

"Thank you so much for this incredibly fun night, Natashia" Mia told her and gave her a big hug. "I really needed it. I felt you somehow already knew that though. So, thank you again."
"You're welcome, sis." She replied.

She was right. A sister. At least what she thought a sister would feel like.

"Drive safe, sis. Text me when you get home, so I know you're safe." She added.

"Will do. You too." Mia replied and gave her one more hug goodbye.

Mia had just pulled in her driveway when she received the notification that Natashia had arrived home safely.

Just pulled in too. Ready for bed. Thanks again for a fun night! Xo Mia replied.

Chapter Twenty-Three

5:30am

Thursday morning before the August long weekend when her alarm went off.

She had taken a couple of extra days to travel up North to her cousins' cottage. She had a few grocery items to pack away in the cooler and then finished packing up her car before taking off.

Mia loved the four-hour drive there because it reminded her of her happier days in her childhood. Her aunt would always bring her, her sister, and their three cousins for a few weeks at the end of every August before they headed back to school.

It became a summer tradition for Mia for as long as she could remember. A hideaway retreat where she was able to regroup and recharge in her adult years.

Mia placed her last item in the passenger seat and messaged her cousin, who was already there waiting for her, to let he know she is on her way. She didn't expect an immediate response since it wasn't even past six o'clock in the morning.

She cranked the tunes and sang her heart out the entire way of the beautiful sunny morning drive.

10:06 am.

Mia made the final tight turns on the long narrow dirt road and was relieved that she never ran into any oncoming cars. There was hardly enough space in some areas for her SUV to pass without brushing against some shrubs, let alone two cars passing through.

Sophia had heard her cousin Mia driving in and waved. Mia had not seen her cousin since the beginning of her separation and was a little nervous about any more judgements she might receive.

Mia got out of her car and her cousin gave her a big hug.

"I'm so glad you made it up here. I wasn't sure you would be coming this year." Said Sophia.

"I wasn't sure either, but knew I had to. I was happy to hear the rental cottage was available." Mia replied and opened her trunk to unpack.

It brought back some memories of her and former husband Jack. He would come with her for many summers. He loved the cottage too.

"I'll let you get settled and come back after to join you. We can hang out at the rental property today." Sophia said.

After unpacking, Mia put on her bikini and went outside and placed her towel down on the grass to relax by the water.

The white rustic rectangular cottage wasn't big and had become pretty run down over the years. Afterall, it was built in the 1960's and hadn't received many updates since it was built.

It was on a piece of land that was picture perfect, tucked away from other cottages. The grass surrounding the cottage met their tiny private beach that gave a view to the entire lake.

She laid on her towel and felt the warm sun hitting her skin. In the distance, she would hear the occasional peaceful calling of a loon singing in the lake before ducking under water and popping it's had up in another location.

12:14 pm

"Ready for a drink?" She heard Sophia ask as she walked towards her with two drinks in her hands.

"Sure! Thanks! Why not. After all, I am on vacation, aren't I?" Mia replied. Her cousin handed her a drink then sat down in a Muskoka chair that was close to Mia.

"How are you?" She asked Mia in a more serious tone.

Mia knew what she was referring to.

She took a deep breath in anticipation of where this conversation might go.

"Better now thanks. It was really hard there for a while. But I found my strength and I am happier than I've been in a long time." Mia confessed.

"I'm not going to lie; it was a shock to us all. We had no idea that you were ever unhappy. If you are happy about your decision, that's all that matters." Sophia added.

"It was the most difficult decision I have ever made in my life. But I am." Mia told her.

"To happiness." Sophia said as they touched their glasses and took a sip.

The sun was beating down on them. They poured themselves another beverage and hopped on some floats and floated away on the water laughing and reminiscing about their childhood.

They both loved to be on the water and were both really good swimmers. Each year Mia went up to the cottage, she would take some time to swim across the lake. Something she loved to do and would always try to beat her previous years' time.

4:32 pm

They were both a little tipsy and getting really hungry. So, they decided to make their way back to the cottage and fire up the barbeque.

6:12 pm

After they filled their tummies, they gathered wood to place around the firepit that was located right beside the water's edge.

This was one of Mia's favourite parts at the cottage. Sitting around the campfire and stargazing on a warm summer's night.

Sophia made a couple more drinks for her and Mia. They sat beside each other in front of the fire. Mia could sit there all day and night, enjoying the tranquility of nature and all its surroundings.

The sun was beginning to settle below the trees, and they watched all the fishermen make their way back to their cottages before it got too dark and could hear the upcoming silence of the night.

They could already see some stars shining their way in the night's sky, so Mia placed a few more logs on the fire before the sun had completely set.

The sky was clear with no clouds in sight, and they could see the depth of all the stars that filled the night sky.

It brought Mia back to the times she spent gazing at the stars with her former husband there and all the late nights they spent together looking for shooting stars.

Each time Mia saw one, she would shout in amazement, "did you see that one?" in hopes her wishes were granted.

Most of her wishes had already come true, but not in the way she ever thought they would.

She learned from her wishes, she had to let faith take its course. To surrender and trust that everything is always working out for her and her desires, even when it appeared otherwise.

"Did you see that shooting star?" Mia asked Sophia after making her wish.

"Ugh, no I missed it." She replied with disappointment.

1:11 am

Mia and Sophia were both getting tired and decided to call it a night. They put out the fire and Mia watched her cousin's flashlight light her way back to her cottage and Mia walked into hers. Alone.

The silence of the night was loud. It was her first time staying there alone. She had a moment of gratitude for all the memories that she shared there with her former spouse and was looking forward to experiencing new ones yet to be created from the wishes she had just made on the shooting star.

Chapter Twenty-Four

7:38 am

Mia heard the chirping of the birds outside her window telling her it was time to get up.

It was another beautiful day and Mia wanted to take full advantage of it.

She put on her workout clothes, made herself a coffee, then walked down to sit on the dock where she could see the sun rising above the tree lines and its reflection that glistened on the water like diamonds.

She took a deep breath and felt the warmth of the sun as though it could enter her heart and wash away any residues of sadness.

The more she connected with her breath work and the warmth glow from the sun, the more peace she felt within.

"Morning! How was your sleep?" She heard Sophia shout from the other cottage. She must have seen Mia sitting on the dock meditating.

"Morning!" Mia shouted back. "It was good. Slept like a baby. Yours?"

"It was good. I'll be over in a minute. When did you want me to take out the canoe to shadow you for your swim across the lake?" Sophia asked.

"Whenever you're ready. Umm, before breakfast preferably, so I don't get a cramp while swimming." Mia told her.

"Ok, give me 20 minutes." Sophia said and saw her disappear to get ready.

Mia went back into the cottage to change into her bathing suit and met up with her cousin down by the dock. Her cousin was accustomed to canoeing alongside Mia's trek across the lake for safety reasons. To make sure the other boaters didn't run her over.

"Ready?" Sophia asked Mia.

"Ready! Time?"

8:49 am

The water was a bit cool on her skin, but Mia knew she would warm up as she got going.

The lake was calm with no currents as she swam towards the middle. There were only a few boaters out around this time since most of the early morning fisherman had already made their way back by now.

When she approached the deeper parts of the lake, Mia's fears would creep up on her, thinking that there was something under her that might get her. She hated not being able to see the depths below or what could be swimming underneath her. Each time a fear would try to sneak in her mind, attempting to stop her, she would redirect her focus on the shoreline.

"Time?" Mia asked Sophia as she touched the rocks across the lake.

"9:04 am. Great job! I think that might be your new record." Sophia exclaimed.

"It is!" Mia replied excitedly. "Give me a minute so I can catch my breath before heading back."

"Take as long as you need." Sophia responded while she floated alongside her.

Mia took a moment to feel how proud she was of herself. All of her hard work and accomplishments, she wasn't doing to prove to anyone else. It was all for her.

"Ready." Mia told Sophia. "Time?"

9:07 am

The current picked up and was now against her, and she felt the waters attempting to push her backwards. Nothing could stop her. At times she felt as though her life was exactly like a current which she was swimming against.

"Time?" Mia asked again.

9:24 am

"Amazing, Mia!" Sophia said with a big smile on her face.

"Meet you at your cottage in about 10 minutes so we can do what we did yesterday?" Sophia asked Mia with a laugh.

"That's what I'm here for! A little rest and relaxation with some drinks along the way." Mia replied.

It was another perfect day to do nothing. Just relax and chill by the waterfront. As Mia settled in her spot, she could hear the laughter of children jumping in the distance off their water trampolines and the sound of motors on the jet skis that were flying across the lake.

"So, have you considered dating anyone new?" Sophia inquisitively asked as she sat down beside Mia.

"Nope. All the guys that have been hitting on me recently are either married, don't want any kind of commitment, or are in their late twenties." Mia laughed as she saw the shock on Sophia's face.

"Seriously! In their late twenties!" Mia repeated. "I mean, it's flattering and all considering I just turned forty-two, but not at all what I am looking for. I mean, I didn't leave a seventeen-year relationship to settle for anyone. I'd rather be alone."

"Wow. Married men? That's just wrong. Guys in their twenties? Wow!" Sophia answered, not sure what to make of it all.

"What I have observed and from the many conversations I have had around my separation, there are so many people in relationships that are unhappy. Yet do nothing about it." Mia replied. "How about a drink?"

"I think I need one after hearing what I just heard." Sophia said and they both laughed.

4:15 pm

"I'm gonna fire up that barbeque now. I'm absolutely starving!" Sophia announced.

They were too busy relaxing and floating around in the lake all day they had forgotten to eat again.

It was another beautiful night without a cloud in the sky. They finished dinner, and once again gathered up some firewood for their nightly fire.

Mia poured some more drinks and grabbed some blankets as the temperature started to fall as the sun set.

Peace enveloped Mia's mind and body as the stars illuminated the clear night's sky.

"Did you see that one?" Sophia asked Mia as she saw a shooting star.

"I did." Mia replied with a smile and finished making yet another wish.

Chapter Twenty-Five

11:07am

As Mia pulled into her driveway early the Sunday morning. She wanted to be sure to beat all the traffic from the long weekend rush as it would have been worse than the daily work commutes.

Another beautiful hot summer day to enjoy, and Mia hadn't made any other plans. She knew her friends were busy or away, so she decided that she would first unpack her car then go for a nice long walk around her neighbourhood.

3:03 pm

Mia put on her running shoes and felt guided to walk to her favourite pond. She could smell barbeques and hear music along her way from the houses that were hosting parties.

She made her way around a secluded part of the neighbourhood leading her to the path that would bring her to her little hideaway.

She crouched close to the water's edge were she saw the same two ducks swimming across the pond every time she was there on her visits.

She heard the voice of a little inquisitive boy coming around the path. He couldn't have been older than three. Mia watched him as he held the hand of a woman that appeared to be his grandmother.

He was firing question after question to her as the elderly lady happily walked hand in hand with him.

She reminded Mia of her grandmother who passed away when she was only eleven years old.

Mia loved her grandmother and sometimes felt her spirit with her throughout the years. She would always remember her grandmother would tell her to breathe and count to ten whenever Mia was upset or angry.

Mia smiled thinking about her and would often talk to her and her grandfather that were together in heaven, asking them for guidance along her way, and would be reassured they were listening when two doves would appear out of nowhere.

Mia stood up to allow the grandmother and grandson to take her place by the water's edge and smile to them as she walked passed them.

She wasn't ready to go home yet, so she kept walking toward the path that looped around the park close to her house.

The park looked extra busy today with people playing all kinds of sports, children sliding down the slides, and swinging from the monkey bars.

She recognized some people from the community and greeted them "hello" as she passed by.

She was then stopped by a familiar face along the trail.

"Hey, how you doing?" Asked Mark.

"I am good thanks. You? Enjoying this beautiful weather, I see." Mia replied.

She had seen Mark many times at their local restaurant. He was always friendly and said hello to Mia whenever they encountered each other. She didn't know too much about him, other than she knew that when he first moved to the area, she would see him eating dinner with another women. Mia assumed it was his wife.

"Yes, I am. Did you hear about the community barbeque they are having here at the park next week?" He asked Mia.

"I thought I heard something about it but wasn't sure if I could make it with work and all." Mia told him.

"Well, maybe I will see you there?" He asked.

"Maybe. My plate is a kinda full right now, but it does sound like

it would be fun." She responded.

"Well, enjoy the rest of you day." He said and continued to walk along the path.

4:48 pm

Mia had just sat on her couch to watch a movie and heard her phone ding with a notification that she had received another text message. It was from Adam.

Hey, thinking of you. Miss you.

He still never added anything further details to his messages or made any plans to see her again.
She felt as though at times she was, in his mind, a marionette puppet. He would occasionally pull her strings and play with her.

His messages would always put her into a contemplative state. Thinking back to their relationship and how it all transpired and feeling the absence of his magnetic force. Like a cat chasing a mouse.

Part of her still wanted to remain friends in hopes that maybe one day he would change. That Adam would come running back to her begging her to return to him and profess his love for her. The love she felt they had towards each other but could not act upon.

Thinking of you. Mia wrote back.

To her surprise, he responded right away saying **I wish I could see you again soon.**

XO was the last text she typed to him, with the same response from him.

Mia shook her head and didn't give it any more thought. Instead, she pressed play on the romantic comedy movie she selected earlier, snuggled under her blankets, and drifted off to sleep.

Chapter Twenty-Six

9:33 am

Mia heard a notification on her phone. She looked, to see who it was. She was surprised to see that it was from Mark, the guy from the restaurant. He must have found her on her social media and sent her a private message.

Curious, she opened the message that had a link attached.

Hey, it was nice running into you yesterday. Here is the info about the barbeque event that is happening in the park I told you about.

She typed back right away.

Thanks for the info! I really appreciate it. I probably won't be going though. I think my former husband will be there. I'd rather not run into him with his new girlfriend and all right now.

You and are in the same boat. He told her.
Oh, I am sorry to hear that. Mia texted back. She had no idea.

It's ok, it's been several months now. All good. What are you up to today? He asked.

I have an event that I have to go to. It's out of town. I am just getting ready now. Have to head out soon. She wrote back.
.
Oh, nice. Which one? He asked.

Something for work. She texted back.

It's a beautiful day. He wrote back.

He wasn't giving up on this conversation, she thought.

Yes, it is. I have to get going and finish getting ready. Thanks again for the info. She typed.

Anytime. Hey, maybe we could get a coffee later? He asked.

I will be out all night. So tonight, won't work. She informed him.

Ok, what about tomorrow? Are you free? He was persistent.

That might work. Let me get back to you tomorrow. Like I said, I am running late now and have to get going. I hope you enjoy the rest of the day. Mia messaged.

You too. Have fun at your event. Was his last text.

Mia liked his message and finished with a happy face emoji.

As she rushed off to her event, she kept thinking about her surprise conversation with Mark and how sweet it was of him to find her on social media and send her all the event info.

She never had any in-depth conversations with Mark other than a wave hello when she saw him around. Mia was curious and wanted to find out more about him and his mysterious vibe she would always pick up on.

She arrived at her event and told her co-worker about the interesting and unusual interaction she had with Mark.

Mia told her co-worker that she sensed that after his mention about his separation, that perhaps he was a little more interested in her than just grabbing a coffee.

11:39 pm

Mia pulled into her driveway after her long day. She was happy as her work event was a huge success but was ready to call it a night.

She quickly got ready for bed and as her head hit the pillow, she thought about Mark and herself saying yes to that potential coffee date with him tomorrow. She was very interested in meeting up with him and already knew her answer would be yes.

Chapter Twenty-Seven

Mia had just got back from her early Saturday morning routine. Meditate, workout, groceries, and clean. She loved her routines. It's what kept her feeling sane and at peace.

10:52 am

She picked up her phone to play some more music from her liked song list so she could dance and sing while she finished off a few more chores.

Just as she was pressing play, a new message from Mark appeared on her phone.

Hey, how was your event last night? He asked.

She smiled and replied. It was good. Thanks for asking. How was the rest of your evening?

Kinda boring lol, just stayed home and watched TV. By myself. He typed.

She could see him typing more from the three dots that appeared on the bottom of the screen.

Did you still want to get together for a coffee later? Say 8:30 pm? He asked.

Not sure about coffee at that time lol but maybe tea? Mia messaged back.

Lol You're right. Kinda late for a coffee. Why don't we meet in the parking lot at the park? He suggested.

Sounds good. I will see you then. She told him.

What kind of tea can I grab for you? He asked her.

Matcha tea with almond milk please. She responded.

Great! Enjoy your day and see you at 8:30 pm in the parking lot. He sent back with a happy face emoji.

She hit the play button on her phone and was filled with excitement about a new possibility of getting to know someone new. He was always polite, and she was getting tired of all the other guys trying to ask her out, and for not the right reasons either. Well, at least from Mia perspective.

Mia was a hopeless romantic and knew in her heart she would fall in love again one day.

6:59 pm

Mia turned off the hot water to her shower and dried off. She wanted to pick out a cute outfit for tonight. She walked over to her closet and opened the double doors and began her search.

Most of her wardrobe were shades of black, grey, white, or beige. She didn't like large or floral patterns. She put on her blue ripped jeans and black tank top and went to her bathroom to do her hair and put on a little makeup. Not too much because she didn't want to feel overdone.

8:27 pm

Mia received a text from Mark saying that he had just parked his car.

She let him know that she was on her way out the door to meet him and would be there in less than five minutes.
Mia hopped in her car and drove the minute drive into the park parking lot where she saw his car parked.

She pulled up alongside the passenger side of his car. Mark smiled and lifted her takeout cup he had bought for her then waved and gestured for her to go into his car.

She hopped out of her driver's seat and opened his car door and closed it.

"Hey" Mia said as she sat down.

"Hey," he said back. "Here's your tea. I hope I got it right?" and repeated her order back to her.

"Sounds like you did. Thanks again." And lifted her tea to cheers his.

"Thanks for meeting me." He said "I wasn't sure you would. I know I have seen you around many times and I heard that you were going through a separation. Thought that since I am too, we could meet up and talk since we see each other around all the time." He said. He seemed a bit nervous. But so was Mia. She really didn't know what to expect.

They each took a sip of their tea, and she could see how spotless his car was. It looked like it had just been detailed, it was so clean.

They exchanged the basic parts of their stories around each other's separation. The basics of what happened. When? Why? Who left who, and how they were both grateful they didn't have any children to go through any of it.

He had a great sense of humour and a kindness about him that she liked, and she could tell by the way he looked at her that he was into her.

They laughed a lot. Something she absolutely loved. To her surprise, he was extremely funny and kept Mia laughing for hours. She was so grateful she said yes to this mini parking lot date she thought.

10:34 pm

"Listen Mark, it's getting late. I know it's the weekend, but I have an early start tomorrow. Thanks for inviting me out to meet you tonight. I had a really fun time with you, and I really enjoyed laughing with you. Thank you again." Mia said and reached over to give him a goodbye hug.

When she started to pull away, he touched the back of her head and pulled her back for a kiss. It caught Mia off guard. Something Mia did not expect at all.

"I better go now," she said with a smile. "Thank you." And kissed him back.
She opened the passenger side door and hopped back into her SVU.

She looked over to him through the car windows. She saw him watching her from the lights that reflected from his dashboard.

She smiled and waved and put her car into reserve.

She couldn't believe what had just happened. She was pleasantly surprised by him. By his wits and his intelligence, she found him to be very sexy.

Chapter Twenty-Eight

8:12pm

Tuesday night Mia opened her front door moments after she heard her doorbell ring. It was Mark. He had been texting her over the past few days, checking in with her to see how her days were going.

They both talked about getting together again to watch a movie, so she invited him to her place.

"Hey," he said, "Nice place."

"Thanks. I'm renting it. For now. Actually, I'm looking to buy a home now. I can't believe it's already almost one year since I have been living here." She informed him. "I'm sure you'll find the right place. Looking to move close by?" He asked.

"Yes. I do really love it here, even though my commute to work can be a pain in the ass sometimes with all the traffic." She laughed.

"Sorry, please come in." She said as she realized they were still standing in her foyer.

Mark laughed. "Thought you changed your mind for a second." He said in a joking manner.

Mia laughed and walked towards the living room.

"Would you like a drink?" Wine?" She asked him.

"Do you have red?" He asked.

"I do." She said and stepped into the kitchen to pour a glass of red for him and a white wine for her. For a second, it reminded her of Adam.

"Here you go." She said while handing him his glass and sitting down on the couch beside him.

"Cheers." He said and lifted his glass to hers.

"Cheers." She replied and they each took a sip together.

Mark oozed a mysterious sexiness vibe.

She put her glass of wine on the coffee table, and when she sat back, he leaned in and kissed her.

She felt a jolt of vibrations course through her body. He stopped to look at her and smirked as if he had intentionally sent this shock wave through her. He placed his glass next to hers.

She felt his hand reach behind her neck and gently, yet firmly pull her neck towards him to kiss her.

Another jolt shot through her.

Their breathing started to get heavy from the sensual touch of his hand running up and down her body. He moved his hand over her chest and squeezed her breast. She pulled him close, letting him know she wanted more.

She felt his hand move down her torse and waist towards her hips. He grabbed her and pulled her pelvis closer to him.

His hands moved into her pants and onto her clit that was covered by her thong. His fingers gently glided up and down over the fabric, sending pleasure through her body.

She grabbed him in approval of his touch, and she felt his tongue moving down in between her legs to meet his hand.

He pulled down her pants. Her thong still intact.

She felt his breath over her thong and slowly pushed it out of the way with his tongue, moving it in circular motions over her clit.

She moaned with contentment and moved her hands to grab the back of his hairless head when he moved his fingers inside of her.

"You taste so good." She heard him speak softly.

He didn't stop until she was done then looked up at her with a sense of pride with his accomplishment that he made her cum.

When he got back up, she grabbed him and forcefully sat him on the couch. He smiled and she started to undue his belt to his pants to return the favour.

Chapter Twenty-Nine

A few months had gone by, Mark and Mia would meet up a few times per week to see each other in secluded locations or at each other's house. It was this sneaky behaviour Mia loved as it reminded her of her teenage years and the times when she didn't want to get caught doing something she wasn't supposed to.

Except this relationship wasn't like that. They were both just tired of the gossip and drama that surrounded their own separations they didn't want to add another story to the mix.

1:22 pm

Mia was out shopping that Friday afternoon. Mark had messaged her asking her how her day was going, and what she was up to.

Just at the mall picking up a few things I needed at one of the stores they have here. She texted back.

Oh, wow seriously? I am just around the corner running errands! Wanna meet in the parking lot? I will be done in about 15 minutes. How about you? He asked.

I can make that work. Let me know where you park, and I will meet you. She replied.

A few minutes later she received his text letting her know where he had parked.

She messaged him back to tell him she would meet him in his car in five minutes.

As she walked through the parking lot, she saw his white car with dark tinted windows parked in one of the corners where they wouldn't be seen.

She opened the passenger door and hopped in his vehicle.

He didn't say a word, nor did she. They looked into each other's eyes and they both smirked. They knew what they both wanted, and it wasn't a conversation. They were hungry for each other. Hungry for more.

He pulled her close with his hand he had placed around the back of her neck and quickly moved his other hand up her skirt to feel inside of her.

She loved how he touched her.

She reached her hand over to remove his pants. They couldn't move fast enough.

He released his hand from inside of her to help speed up the process to pull down his own pants.

As he exposed himself, she leaned in and put her lips and mouth around him.

They fed off the thrill of trying not to get caught.

When they were both satisfied, he pulled his pants back up and they gazed at each other with a smile on each of their faces.

"Listen, let's plan a night where you come over for dinner to my place. We can order in like we did the last time I went over to your house." He suggested.

"I would love to." She answered back "This week is a bit hectic for me. My lease on my rental place is up as you know, and I am waiting to hear back about the offer I put on that house. How does next Monday sound?"

"Yes, actually that day works for me too. I'll put it in my calendar." He answered.

"Ok then. Next Monday it is." She confirmed.

Chapter Thirty

2:13pm

Mia pulled into the local café to meet with her girlfriend named Joy for some Matcha teas. It was their usual meeting place.

Joy had been in Mia's life for over a decade now but had been going through many of her own challenges and took some time to herself. They had drifted apart for a few years, not because they didn't like each other, but because they were both dealing with so much upheaval in their own lives.

Mia adored Joy and appreciated her brutal honesty with her. Whether she agreed or disagreed with Mia, Joy was always able to give her a different perspective on life without judging her. They grabbed their order and sat on some comfy taupe couches to chat and catch up.

Just as Mia was about to take her first sip, her phone rang. It was her realtor.

"Hello." Mia answered in a nervous voice.

"Hi Mia, it's Russell, I wanted to let you know that all the paperwork has gone through. You are moving in less than three weeks! Congratulations! The house is all yours!"

Mia was stunned. She couldn't believe what she had just heard. The wonderful news was that she was now a homeowner. All her hard work had paid off.

It was a difficult process for her to buy this home, for she was required to provide the mortgage company with a legal document indicating that she was indeed separated for her to be approved. However, her former husband had still not disclosed his financial documents and was holding everything up. She still needed her separation to be finalized and was unable to submit the correct documents.

Mia thought her ex would have wanted to speed up the process, especially after she found out he had been dating one of her old friends from twenty years during the last several months. It wasn't a surprise to Mia. She had a vision of the two of them together, and even told him about when they were just separating.

Thankfully, the mortgage company agreed to an affidavit and Mia was able to obtain his signature to receive the approval.

Joy had a big smile on her face. She could hear Mia's good news and excitement before she got off the phone.

"Oh my god, thank you so much Russell for all your help and this incredible news!" she said as tears of joy streamed down her face.

"Congratulations again. You deserve it. I'll send over all the final paperwork in a few minutes. Enjoy the rest of your day and I will be in touch with you later on." He added.

As Mia pressed end on her phone, they both jumped up from their chairs and Joy gave Mia the biggest hug.

"Congratulations Mia," Joy said. "You got this. It's all coming together for you. You have overcome so much. Now look at all the good that is coming into your life. What do you want to do to celebrate later?"

"Oh, well, um, actually I have a date with some guy I have been kinda seeing. We have been having little secret rendez-vous and it's actually been fucking amazing! I feel like a kid again when I am with him!" Mia blurted out.

"What? You never told me this. When did this happen?" She quickly asked wanting to know every single detail.

Mia laughed nervously "Um, well, a few months ago now. Sorry, we weren't going to say anything to anyone. I really didn't know where it was all going. It just kinda happened, and it has been happening. All I know is that I am having so much fun with him."

"Well, that's amazing! I am so happy for you! When you're ready to spill the beans with all the details let me know!" Joy said eagerly hoping Mia would tell her more.

"Well, I think I will be picking up a bottle of champagne to celebrate with him tonight. He's going to order some dinner at his place. He has something planned for us." Mia said excitedly.

"Well, I would love to take you out to dinner another night to celebrate too. We'll figure it out another time." Said Joy.

"Yes. I better get going so I can pick up some bubbly." Mia told Joy and gave her a hug goodbye.

Just as she left, Mia received a text from Mark. **Still on for tonight? Say 7:30 pm?**

Mia confirmed that she would be there and that she had exciting news to share with him.

She couldn't wait to celebrate with him. She finally felt as though things had started to really come together in her life for the first time in years.

7:32 pm

Mia texted Mark to let him know that she had just pulled up in front of his house.

As she grabbed the bottle of champagne from the back of her car, she saw Mark open the front door.

He smiled and said hello with an inquisitive look on his face as he saw the bottle of champagne.

"What are we celebrating?" He asked.

She walked up his two front stairs and onto his porch. He held the door open for her.

"I received the best news ever today!" She said and kissed him hello.

"Let me guess," he kissed her back "You got your house?" He questioned.

"I did! I am so proud of myself, and I figured since I was coming here tonight, we could celebrate with a little bubbly." She said happily.

"Congratulations, Mia. I am so happy for you. I know you said it wasn't an easy process." He said and gave her a hug and kiss.

"No, but it all worked out in the end." She smiled and they walked into the kitchen to pour themselves each a glass of champagne.

They sat down on his dark grey sofa, and he kept looking at her as though he had something to say. "What it is?" She asked.

He leaned over to kiss her, then took her hand.

"Come with me." He whispered and led her upstairs.

When they got to the upstairs landing, he covered her eyes with his hands before they entered his bedroom.

She smiled because she had a feeling, he was going to show her something they had been talking about through text messages.

He stood behind her and put his other hand around her waist. She could feel his excitement through his pants when he placed his body up against hers.

"I wanted to surprise you." he said and gently removed his hand that was covering her eyes.

She looked and saw four straps that were attached to all for corners of the bed. Two for her arms and two for her legs.

It was perfect, she thought.

He turned her back to face him and held her close to her body. He started kissing her while he slowly walked her backwards towards the bed.

He laid her down gently on her back and got on top of her.

He slowly took off her black dress and saw that underneath she was wearing a black lace bustier with a matching thong.

He smiled with approval and reached over to his nightstand to place a blindfold over her eyes.

"Alexa, play my music list." She heard him say and heard the music start playing over the speakers in his room.

She felt him breathe in her ear and lightly kiss her right earlobe and side of her neck, gradually moving down towards her breasts.

He then took her hands and guided her arms outwards where she felt him firmly grab each wrist and tie her up.

His soft sensual kisses moved back towards her breast where he then lowered her bustier and licked her nipples.

She didn't resist anything he did and loved him teasing her. In fact, this was something she craved for.

He licked and kissed her, making his way downwards even further. He spread her legs wide open with his hands and she felt him tease her clit with his tongue over her thong. He then moved towards her inner thighs where he took each ankle and secured them to the ankle cuffs.

Mia laid there completely vulnerable and available for him, wanting to feel all of him. The more time she spent with him, the more she desired his touch. It was though he intuitively knew exactly what she wanted, in each moment. It was like he could read her mind and how she wanted to be touched.

Her senses, heightened to his touch, felt him slowly making his way back up her legs. He kissed every inch of her body and teased her upper inner thighs. Wanting her to beg him for more.

"God, you look so hot lying here right now." She heard him say under the music that had become in synch with each of his movements.

She felt his lips with the heat of his breath close to her clit, taunting her again.

"I want to feel you inside of me." She urged him under her heavy breath.

She felt him gently move her thong to the side with his fingers as his lips touched hers.

She moaned again with pleasure. What she had yearned for was happening.

"Oh, Mark!" She yelled.

"Mmm, you taste so good." She heard him say. He then moved his lips back toward her breasts and sucked on her nipples some more.

Mia wanted to touch him so badly but was confined by the ropes that held her entire body to his bed.

He moved his kisses further up to her neck and she felt his hips move between her legs and his hard cock slip inside of her.

"Ohhhh, you feel so good." She heard him say as he moved in a slow, teasing in and out motion.

Mia desired him more and more with his sensual touches and teasing behaviours.

"Fuck me!" Mia demanded.

"You want me?" he asked as he whispered in her ear.

Her senses were so heightened she could hardly take it anymore.

"I want you to fuck me. Hard!" She begged again and just then Mark started fucking her with passionate intent.

"Oh, Mia." He groaned.

They were both moaning for each other as she felt him penetrate deeper inside of her.

They could no longer resist, and they climaxed in unison.

"Oh my god! That was incredible!" She said to him as he took off her blindfold and looked in her eyes.

"You liked that?" He asked with a smirk on his face.

"God I've been wanting to tie someone up for so long." He admitted as he began to untie her.

"That was perfect. Even the music." She told him.

"I made that playlist for us. I thought those songs would be perfect for this moment." He confessed.

He handed back her black dress and gave her another kiss.

"Thank you for this. I really enjoyed it." Mia told him with a smile and gave him one more kiss.

Chapter Thirty-One

Mia was excited as she had packed the final boxes from her rental property. She was just waiting for her lawyer to call to let her know when the keys would be ready to be picked up for her new home.

She was so proud of herself. All her hard work, dedication, and accomplishments she had attained these past fifteen months.

She had achieved success in her new career, made incredible new friends, and now, she was moving into a new home. A home she was able to buy, all on her own.

She was finally feeling happy with her life and who she had become and who she was still thriving to become.

1:02pm

The phone rang. It was the receptionist from her lawyer's office.

"Congratulations Mia, all the final steps are now complete. You can come and pick up your key anytime now.

"Thank you! I will be there in about fifteen minutes or so." She told her.

Mia couldn't wait another minute to get her keys for her home. She quickly grabbed her purse and went straight to the lawyer's office.

On her way she received a text from Mark asking her how her closing was going.

She told him that she was on her way to pick up the keys as they spoke.

Great, I'll have time to come tomorrow to have a look at it. I am so happy for you. Congratulations again Mia. He wrote.

Thank you! I will be around all day tomorrow cleaning and getting the place ready. So come whenever you get a work break. She responded. She arrived at the lawyer's office and picked up her envelope that had her house keys in it and drove right away to her new place.

She video tapped herself opening the door to her new place as walked in. Tears of relief and happiness immediately fell down her cheeks. She had never felt prouder of herself than in that moment.

She wanted to share her news with the world and posted it on social media with the caption, *when one door closes, another one opens,* with a video of her closing the door to her rental property and then opening the door to a home that was now hers.

Her post was also to inspire others along her way, for them to know that anything is truly possibly when they believe in themselves and their dreams.

She stood in her new living room and soaked it all in as she wanted to imprint this memory into her mind forever.

Her phone started buzzing with congratulations messages from her friends and followers.

Her phone notified her once more of another private message. It was from Adam. **Hey Mia, congratulations on your home. I am so proud of you. I have followed you every day on your IG stories. You have come so far. Xo.**

She was happy to hear from him and even though she was seeing Mark. She too would follow him on his stories to see where life was bringing him.

She responded with a thank you and asked how he was doing.

She looked around her place and it already felt like home. That she was somehow guided to this home for a reason. A new chapter in her journey. Another starting point for her to grow and expand even more.

Chapter Thirty-Two

5:00 am

Mia had a hard time sleeping. She was still excited from the day before but had to go to work for a few hours first thing in the morning. She wanted to get back as soon as she could so she could start bringing some boxes over to her new place.

On her way home from work, the cold rain started to pick up and her commute was taking longer than usual. There must had been a car accident up ahead as the traffic was busier than usual at this time. She was now coming to a standstill.

As she sat there, stuck in traffic, she began to reminisce about Adam again. She was stopped close to where she would meet up with him when he stayed here. She thought about the first time they met on that rainy night in his car.

Just then, her phone rang. She was shocked to see the name Adam displayed on her Bluetooth in her car. She couldn't believe the synchronicities.

"Hello." Mia said in a surprised tone.

"Hi Mia, I know it's been a while, but I just wanted to call you this time and tell you how proud I am of you. I have been thinking about you so much lately, of us, and how much I miss you. I have been watching your posts and when you posted about your new home, I knew I had to reach out. You see, I wanted to make sure I wasn't a rebound for you at the time you left your marriage. I was so drawn to you, and I got so scared of getting hurt. I had to hold back. Sorry, I know that was a lot, but I have been waiting for the right moment to tell you how I felt." He blurted out.

Mia was silent as she was taking in every word he said.

"Hello? You there?" He asked.

"Yes, sorry, it's just crazy. I'm sitting here, stuck in traffic, and I was literally thinking of you just now. I'm stopped close to where you stayed when you came here to work. It's pouring rain and I was thinking about the first time we sat in your car in the rain. Then you called." She confessed.

"I will never forget that night. You were so nervous" He added with a little laugh.

"I was. And you sat there staring at me while you were so calm. I was totally freaking out inside. So much was happening in my life at that time." She confirmed. "Do you still have that picture from that night?" She asked as she remembered he took a picture of her sitting in his car. Mia hated it because she looked like she was a deer caught in headlights.

"I do." He said. "Listen, I really want to see you. And now with you having your new place and all, I want to fly out and spend some time with you. Once you're settled of course."

Just then, she received another call on her other line. It was Mark.

12:17 pm

"Adam, I am sorry, I have another call, let me call you back." Mia said quickly.

"Take your time. Mia, I love you." He said and he hung up the phone.

She couldn't believe her ears. She always felt that he loved her. But everything between them, their distance apart, his in-and-out behaviour seemed too complicated.

She picked up the other line.

"Hey Mia, how's your day going?" Mark asked her with excitement.

She was still in shock from what had just transpired with Adam and tried to gather her thoughts.

"Um, good, other than being stuck in traffic. Yours?"

"Good, I should be wrapping up work in a couple of hours. Let me know when you are home, and I can stop by if you still want me to?" He asked.

"I would love to show you my new place. I'll send you a message when I get home." She let him know.

"Ok, great. Drive safe. Hopefully this rain stops soon." He added. "Talk soon." And he hung up.

Rain, she thought. *That rainy night where it all started months ago with Adam.*

2:03 pm

Mia pulled into her driveway from her extra-long commute from a car accident that had blocked two lanes on the highway.

She texted Mark right away letting her know she had just pulled up to her new place.

I'm just wrapping things up on my end at work before my next meeting. I can pop over around 2:45 pm if that is, ok? He asked.

Yup, come over whenever. I'll be around. She replied.

Mia spent the next little while walking back and forth from her car to her bedroom, loading and unloading boxes with her clothes, some towels, and blankets.

She heard the doorbell ring just as she placed her last box upstairs. *It must be Mark* she thought with a smile and quickly made her way down the wooden staircase.

She opened the door and saw Mark standing outside with a big smile on his face.

"This is great, congratulations again." He said.

"Thank you," Mia said with a giant grin on her face. "Please come in, I can't wait to show you around!"

Her two-story townhome wasn't very big but with an open concept, tall ceilings, and large windows gave it an even larger appearance.

Mia walked him down the narrow corridor to her kitchen that was off to the right, and her living room to the left.

"This is perfect for you." Mark added.

"I know, I am really going to love it here. I feel it." She shared. "Let me show you the upstairs." And walked him back towards the front entrance and up the staircase.

There were two bedrooms to the back of her house with her bedroom that overlooked the front driveway.

"This is my room, "Mia said with outstretched arms.

Mark walked up to her and kissed her.

"I want to be the first one to christen your home with you." He said and reached for one of her blankets that was tucked away in the corner to spread it out on the floor.

He pulled her towards him and lightly touched her face and kissed her.

Their yearning for each other was strong as their busy schedules kept them apart these last few weeks.

He guided her body to the floor and took off pants.

She missed his touch and was grateful to celebrate this moment with him.

Chapter Thirty-Three

It was getting close to Christmas and Mia was almost already settled in her home. She had already painted most of the rooms in the first couple of weeks of moving in. It was another form of therapy for Mia.

She was still seeing Mark, but with their busy schedules, not as much as she would have hoped for, and looked forward to seeing him later that night at her place.

It had already been four months since they were seeing each other, and she had started to have feelings for him. He had come into her unexpectedly and she was really enjoying her time with him.

That night, Mia wanted to solidify their relationship and progress things further with him.

3:47 pm

Mia was cleaning up around her house and getting ready for the evening when she received a notification on her phone.

She picked it up and read, I **really want to come visit. I don't know when yet. But my energy is one hundred percent about it. You are so beautiful and sexy, and I love our bodies together. I love and adore you.**

It was from Adam. She hadn't received a message from me in about a week or two, but he was starting to be persistence again. Every time he would message her, she felt that little magnetic pull again toward him.

Mia still hadn't told Adam about Mark. There was always this yo-yo affect with him and she felt as though that relationship gave her whiplash at times with his in and out behaviour. But she did think of him often and would still wonder at times what if...

Would love to catch up soon. She responded. She had so much she wanted to tell him.

Mia finished her cleaning and hopped in the shower to shave and get ready for her rendezvous with Mark.

She wasn't sure what to wear. She wanted something comfy and casual since he was coming over after dinner because he had to work late again. It was the only time he could come these last couple of weeks.

She put on a cute pair of grey track pants without any panties, a black push-up sports bra and a fitted tank top which showed off her cleavage. She put on a little makeup and put her hair in a cute little bun.

8:13 pm

A message came through her phone letting her know he was outside.

She opened her front door and as he walked in, he gave her a kiss.

"I've missed you." She told him.

"Ya, sorry, I've just been so busy with work." He answered.

"Would you like something to drink?" She asked.

"Just a water please." He responded politely.

They sat on her couch. They got caught up with their last couple of days, but she was a little too distracted to say much. He was so sexy to Mia and since she hadn't seen him in a few weeks, all she could think about was him inside of her.

He took a sip of his water and as he put the glass down, she got on top of him and straddled his lap. There was something so sultry about the way he kissed that it kept her wanting more.

She felt his hand firmly grab her ass to assist her up and down motions.

"You're not wearing anything underneath, are you?" he asked her with a grin on his face.

"Nope. Trying to eliminate a step or two. I missed you and wanted you badly." She confessed.

He flipped her off him and turned her around. He stood up to move behind her. He pulled down her pants and bent her over her couch to enter her from behind.

Mia moaned as he thrusted inside of her. She felt his hand reach around to grab her firmly by the front of her neck. Something she learned to love with him.

She groaned again and she felt him deep inside of her as he smacked her ass.

She couldn't stop her sensation and quickly gave in to her orgasm which made her call out his name, forcing him to succumb to his weakness for her.

"My god I enjoy you fucking me." she proclaimed.

"Me too." He agreed as they both put their clothes back on and sat on the couch.

Mark took another sip of his water, and he noticed Mia looking at him.

"What are you thinking? I can tell you are thinking about something. What is it?" Mark insisted.

"Well, I've been thinking, you know we have been kinda seeing each other for a few months now, and I wanted to check in to see where you are at." She expressed.

"Where I am at with what?" He questioned.

"With us. I really like you. I think you're amazing and I want to start to move towards the next level with you." she admitted.

"Listen, Mia I really like hanging out with you and all, but I am not ready for any commitments. What's wrong with what we have? I just want to have fun. Aren't we having fun?" He asked Mia,

"We are. And that's the thing. It's been incredible these past few months together. I thought that maybe you would want to too." She wondered.

"I'm sorry, it's just where I'm at right now. I don't want to have any commitments. I'm still not ready." He told her.

She felt her heart sink.

"If that's how you feel, I respect that. But I also have to respect how I feel. It doesn't seem like we are on the same page, and I want to be with someone who is. I get where you're at and I don't want to pretend that I feel otherwise. I have to honour how I feel too." She said.

"I wish we were on the same page, but maybe we should take a step back from each other right now." He suggested.

"I guess that's we'll have to do." Mia sadly agreed.

"I am sorry if I ever mislead you. I don't want to hurt you. It's just how I feel and where I am at right now." He reaffirmed.

"And I respect that. I have loved every second with you and all the fun we have had together and exploring new parts of my sexuality with you. Really, I am so grateful for you." Said Mia.

"Me too." He agreed. "We've explored a lot together. Me too, I am grateful, but I guess I should get going. It's getting late."

"You're right, it is late, and we both have to be up early for
work. Let me walk you to the door," she said.

He put his shoes on and gave her one more kiss before he left.

"Good night. I'll talk to you in the morning." He told her but she knew she would not receive her usual good morning text from him.

She watched him get into his car and drove off.

Chapter Thirty-Four

A week had gone by, and she did not hear from Mark. She saw him drive by and wave at her a couple of times while she was out either walking or running around their neighbourhood.

She was so grateful for him as he helped her awaken a sensual side of her, she didn't even know existed. But she wasn't the type to beg anyone to stay. Mia knew that when it was time to let them go, to release them.

Mia went back into Hermit mode and started focusing on herself again. She was feeling good about the direction in her life and where she was going.

Of course, she was sad that things didn't move forward with Mark the way she had hoped for, but she also knew this was another opportunity for her to focus inward on herself so she can achieve her wildest dreams of becoming a famous writer.

It was the universe's way of letting her know that that another cycle had come to a close. To make way for something new to enter her life.

She looked to check the time on her phone. A new message appeared.

I still love you forever Mia, xo.

It always amazed her how the Universe worked. As her and Mark ended things, she felt the magnetic pull from Adam coming back. She knew it was only a matter of time before he would reappear.

She paused for a moment and took a deep breath. A moment to tune into what her heart truly felt about him.

Could they no longer repel the electric impulses. Was the Universe trying to push them back together?

Mia glanced down at her hand and focused on the ring she bought the first time she went to Colorado. She was brought back to the moment with Adam. Brought back to the happiness she felt with him and began to type...

When you called me that last time and told me for the first time that you loved me, I was completely taken back. It was something I wanted to hear from you since the moment we met, and you had asked me if I believed in love at first sight. I am sorry that I held back all this time, but like you, I can no longer deny what I have felt for you. Adam, I love you too.

She did love him. From the moment she saw him. She had been truly grateful for him coming into her life. And, like a tornado, helped her deconstruct her old ways so she could step into who she was always meant to be.

Love & Light,

Sarah

xo.

@iamsarahharper
iamsarahharper.com

Manufactured by Amazon.ca
Bolton, ON

34450967R00151